This book belongs to:

First published in Great Britain in 2022 by Farshore
An imprint of HarperCollins*Publishers*
1 London Bridge Street, London SE1 9GF

farshore.co.uk

HarperCollins*Publishers*
1st Floor, Watermarque Building, Ringsend Road
Dublin 4, Ireland

Text copyright © Katie and Kevin Tsang 2022
Illustration copyright © Amy Nguyen 2022

The moral rights of the authors and illustrator have been asserted

ISBN 978 0 7555 0016 1

Printed and bound in the UK using 100% renewable electricity at
CPI Group (UK) Ltd

1

A CIP catalogue record for this title is available from the British Library.

MIX
Paper from
responsible sources
FSC FSC™ C007454
www.fsc.org

KATIE & KEVIN TSANG

ILLUSTRATED BY AMY NGUYEN

SPACE BLASTERS

SUZIE SAVES THE UNIVERSE

farshore

For Evie and Mira,
we love you more than anything
in the entire universe.

CONTENTS

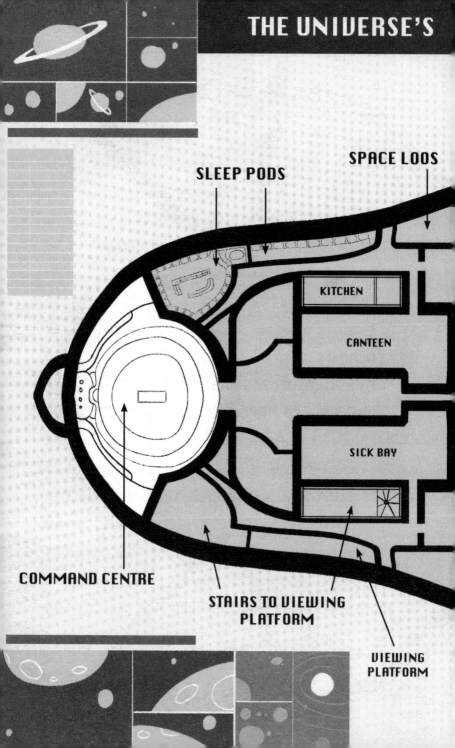

THE UNIVERSE'S

SLEEP PODS

SPACE LOOS

KITCHEN

CANTEEN

SICK BAY

COMMAND CENTRE

STAIRS TO VIEWING PLATFORM

VIEWING PLATFORM

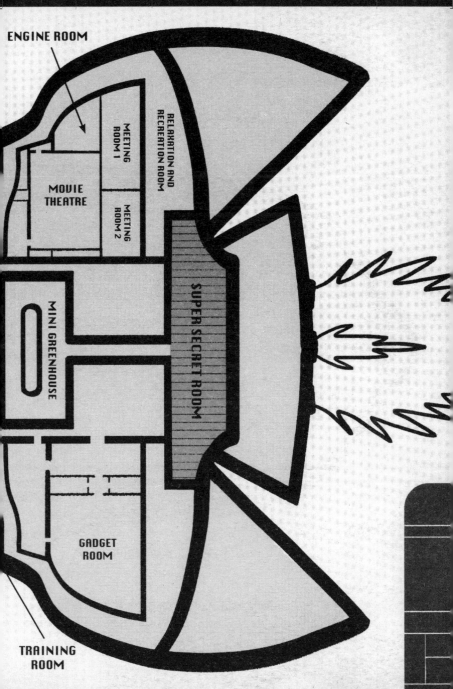

ENGINE ROOM

MEETING ROOM 1

RELAXATION AND RECREATION ROOM

MOVIE THEATRE

MEETING ROOM 2

SUPER SECRET ROOM

MINI GREENHOUSE

GADGET ROOM

TRAINING ROOM

CHAPTER 1

THE EXPLODING DUMPLING MAKER

Have you ever had a really great idea that you just can't hold in? That explodes out of you?

That happens to me *all the time.*

I, Suzie Wen, am full of good ideas. Brilliant ideas even. So full of them that they pop out of me when I least expect it.

In my head, the ideas are perfect. All of my experiments go as planned. My inventions work beautifully.

But for some reason, when I try to make

my ideas a reality, things tend to get a little . . . messy. There was the Great BedMaker malfunction (got stuck in the blankets),

the Hair Detangler disaster (nearly left me bald),

and the FibFinder fiasco (the special serum I concocted turned my mouth blue for a month. *And* it didn't even work).

My most mouth-watering invention was no exception . . .

A very important fact about me is that my favourite food in the whole wide world is dumplings. Specifically Chinese dumplings. I love tiny dumplings that I can gobble up two at a time. I love shrimp dumplings where the rice-paper wrapper is so thin you can see through it. I love dumplings filled with hot soup that spills out when you take a bite and you have to slurp it up. I love sweet, chewy dumplings full of black sesame. I love steamed dumplings, fried dumplings, dumplings big and small. I could eat dumplings all day long and still want more.

My grandma, who I call Po-Po, makes the very best dumplings in the world. I love it when she comes over and shows

me how to make them. First she makes
the filling with pork, chestnuts, soy sauce,
sesame oil, ginger, garlic and chives, and
then we sit at our big kitchen table and put
the filling in the dumpling wrappers. This
is the hardest part, folding the dumpling
wrappers around the filling. You can't
overstuff them, or they'll explode when
they cook. My po-po can fold them into any
shape! She can make ones that look like
little purses, or triangle, folded dumplings,
or ones that look like crescent moons. It
takes me five minutes just to make one,
but she can make twenty dumplings in five
minutes! And mine never look as good as
hers do – but they still taste delicious.

My sister Lizzie and brother David used
to help fold the dumplings too, but now
David spends most of his time in the

garage practising his drums and Lizzie
is always out with her friends. David is
thirteen and Lizzie is fifteen, and they both
love telling me how I'll understand things
when 'I'm older'. My po-po never says that
to me, and she's way older than them!

After we finish folding the dumplings, my
gung-gung (grandpa) either fries them in
hot oil or steams them in a bamboo basket.
He and my po-po always work as a team.
She folds the dumplings and he cooks them.

When we have a mountain of dumplings
ready to eat, my gung-gung challenges me
to a dumpling-eating contest.

'Suzie, I bet you can eat . . . ten
dumplings,' he'll say, picking up his first
dumpling with his chopsticks. 'And I can eat
twelve.'

'Ten! I can eat ten dumplings in one

minute! I bet I can eat . . . sixteen! At least!'

And then we sit at the table and dip our dumplings in chilli sauce so spicy it makes my lips tingle and we eat as many as we can, until I'm so stuffed with dumplings I feel like I might turn into one.

*

I only see my grandparents once or twice a month. They used to live near us, but a few years ago they moved to a village by the sea. My family used to go to dim sum every Sunday in Chinatown and it was the best because I could get all of my favourite dumplings, but now my parents and my brother and sister are all too busy.

Wait, why was I talking about dumplings? Oh yeah! Because I was telling you about my most mouth-watering invention. Which of course has to do with dumplings.

After my grandparents moved, I needed another way to satisfy my dumpling cravings. So I did what I always do.

I solved the problem.

Every problem has a solution, you just have to figure it out!

I knew we had all of the ingredients for dumplings in our kitchen. And I knew that I had all the parts I needed to make a dumpling-making machine. It was just a matter of putting everything together.

My parents are big believers that if something breaks, instead of throwing it away, you fix it. And if you can't fix it, you put it in the garage just in case you need it one day.

This comes in very handy for my inventions. For example, currently in my garage there two busted microwaves, one old rice cooker, three old TV sets, two radios, five broken piano keyboards (this is more to do with my brother who thinks he is a rock star – he has a corner he claims is 'his studio' but it is just the far side of the garage), one archaic lawn mower that looks like an instrument of torture, and of course Flipper.

Flipper is the car that my dad thought he could convert into a WaterCar™. Flipper had one glorious swim . . .

And then it sank.

What made this more stressful is that we were all *inside* Flipper, because my dad was so convinced it would work.

And for about thirty seconds, it did work. Until it didn't. Luckily we all had life jackets on and my mum very wisely insisted that we keep the windows rolled down 'just in case'. It was a good lesson in being prepared for unexpected outcomes.

Although I guess it wasn't

FUN FACT!

The WaterCar is a real car – a combination of a speedboat and a car. It can do 70–80mph on land and over 40mph on water!

that unexpected. There is a reason that there aren't more cars that double as boats.

Now Flipper doesn't work as a car *or* a boat, but my dad can't bear to take it apart. Now me . . . I have no problem borrowing parts from Flipper when I need them. But I know my dad is 'unreasonably attached' to Flipper, so I never take anything *too* obvious.

And I really hope my dad never looks under the bonnet.

So using one of the microwaves, a few wires from Flipper, and a couple of kitchen items that I borrowed and totally meant to return, plus my drill and a few screws, I was able to build the world's first Automatic Dumpling Maker (or ADM, as I called it). I knew it was going to make me rich and famous. Who wouldn't want dumplings on demand?

I was so impressed with myself, I immediately had to try it out. It only made one kind of dumpling, and it was pretty doughy and not the best dumpling I'd ever had, if I'm being honest, but the important thing is that it worked.

Until I tried to make one too many dumplings all at once, and ADM exploded. The explosion shattered a window *and* covered the kitchen in dough and minced pork. And in extremely unfortunate timing, my sister Lizzie was in the kitchen making a cup of tea when it happened. And she was hit in the face with exploding dumpling. From the way she screamed you would have thought her hair had lit on fire. But trust me, she was *totally* fine.

I could tell my parents were secretly impressed with what I'd built, but they still banned me from building any new inventions for a whole month. My dreams of having dumplings on demand were shattered.

But that didn't stop me from my next great invention. The one that changed everything . . .

CHAPTER 2

INTRODUCING THE SUPER 3-D TV GIZMO!

Being banned from building new inventions wasn't even the worst thing in the world.

I knew that because the worst thing had already happened.

Right at the start of summer, my best friend Bonnie moved away. And not just to the seaside like my grandparents did, which would have meant that maybe I could see her once or twice a month.

No. Bonnie moved across the ocean to New York City. If I was lucky I might get to see her once a year.

Bonnie and I have been best friends since even before we were born. That might sound impossible, but our mums were friends when they were pregnant with us, and apparently when they saw each other we would both kick inside our mums' tummies. Already excited to hang out.

Now Bonnie might as well live in a different galaxy, she's so far away.

And it was summertime so I couldn't even see any sort-of friends at school who might become real friends if I tried hard enough.

I asked if I could go stay with Gung-Gung and Po-Po by the sea but they'd gone to Hong Kong to visit relatives there and wouldn't be back for months.

I was stuck at home *all* summer. With no

friends and with a family who was so busy with their own things I might as well have been invisible.

*

Just because I couldn't build any inventions, didn't mean I couldn't *think* about them. I carried my **Idea Notebook** everywhere with me. Because you never know when a Really Great Idea might hit.

I was sitting in the living room by myself, doodling in my notebook while watching an episode of *Space Blasters*. *Space Blasters* is a show about Spaceman Jack, Captain Jane, their alien friend Five-Eyed Frank and all the adventures they have while trying to save the universe. I used to watch it with my brother David before he decided he was too cool for it. But I still like it.

The thing I like about *Space Blasters*

is that no matter what, the crew always has each other's back. They know they can depend on each other. And at the end of each episode, they always save the universe.

All I wanted was to escape for a little bit – to pretend I wasn't spending my summer all by myself. I wanted a summer of adventure. And reading books and watching TV shows helped with that, but I wanted to take it to the next level.

I wanted a 3-D experience. More than 3-D! I wanted to really feel like I was on the Space Blasters' ship, helping the crew save the universe. I wanted to be able to give Spaceman Jack a high five and help Captain Jane fix things on TUBS (that is the

name of their spaceship, it stands for
The Universe's Best Spacecraft). I knew it
was just a TV show, but for one afternoon,
I wanted to pretend it was real.

I leaned back on our old sofa and studied
the TV. Maybe I could make it *feel* more
real . . .

I still technically wasn't supposed to be
building any new inventions – it had only
been two weeks since the ADM explosion
– but I thought I could at least figure
out what parts I would need. It isn't like
anybody was going to notice. Lizzie was out
shopping with her friends, David was at a
music festival, my mum was in her office
with a stack of research books blasting
classical music, and my dad was marking
papers in the garden. He might actually
have been napping. Hard to tell behind his

sunglasses. Nobody would notice if I snuck into the garage just to see what I *maybe* could use for my next invention.

And I was totally going to stop there, I promise! But one thing led to another and the next thing I knew I'd found all the pieces that I needed for the Super 3-D TV Gizmo. The last step was to try and connect it all to the TV.

If my theory was correct, once I plugged it in, the show would blast out around me as a 3-D experience, almost like virtual reality, and I would feel like I really was in it.

And surely *testing* it to make sure it worked didn't count as Actual Inventing?

The TV was still on. It was a new episode of *Space Blasters*, one I'd never seen before.

Spaceman Jack looked out at me from

the TV and smiled. I smiled back (even though I knew he couldn't see me). Captain Jane flipped a switch on TUBS. 'Ready for blast off,' she announced. And I felt like she was talking directly to me.

'**FOR THE UNIVERSE!**,' I said to myself as I plugged in the Super 3-D TV Gizmo.

I held my breath and waited. At first, nothing. And then the screen went fuzzy. Oh no! I whacked the top of the TV. Come on!

'Hello?' Captain Jane's voice echoed through the room. 'Is this thing working?'

I felt my shoulders slump. I could have asked myself the same thing.

The Super 3-D TV Gizmo was a failed experiment. Oh well. I wasn't supposed to be building inventions anyway. With a sigh, I reached out and tugged on the wires to disconnect them.

I frowned. They were stuck.

That was *weird.*

I pulled again, harder this time.

'Preparing for launch,' said Captain Jane.

'Righty-ho!' replied Spaceman Jack.

Their voices sounded louder than they should be. Maybe I'd done something weird to the TV volume? I'd fix it in a second. Right now I needed to unplug these wires and make sure I hadn't broken the TV. David and Lizzie would really be mad at me then.

'Come *on*,' I muttered. 'Just. Unplug!'

I put my foot on the bottom of the TV for leverage and pulled as hard as I could.

'Captain Jane, watch out!' cried Five-Eyed Frank.

There was a loud **BANG** and then a **WHOoOoSH!**

And

everything

went

dark.

CHAPTER 3

AN UNEXPECTED RESULT

'Is it alive?'

Something poked me in the side. I blinked. There was bright light everywhere, and my vision was blurry. I blinked again.

'Argh! It's moving!' There was a scuffle next to my head. 'I can see it moving with ALL of my eyes!'

'Spaceman Jack, can you deal with the unexpected visitor, please?' said a new voice. 'I need to focus on getting us out of this volcano!'

'You betcha! I'll tie it up and we can deal with it later. Right now we've got bigger fish to fry!'

Fish? Volcano? *Spaceman Jack?*

'Wait!' I croaked out. 'Don't tie me up!' I tried to sit up and as I did my vision came into focus. And then I screamed.

Because staring right at me was a huge green ALIEN with five eyes!

Wait a second. I recognised that alien.

'You're Five-Eyed Frank!'

'IT KNOWS MY NAME!' shouted Five-Eyed Frank. His five eyes darting in all directions.

Suddenly another familiar face loomed over me. Perfectly styled blonde hair, with a curly swoosh in the front. Blue eyes that were currently narrowed at me suspiciously. Square jaw. Big white teeth, like the kind you see in toothpaste adverts.

'Spaceman Jack?' I blurted out.

The man I suspected was Spaceman Jack jumped back. 'Thundering asteroids! It knows my name too!'

'WE'VE GOT A SPY ON THE SHIP!' wailed Five-Eyed Frank.

'Will you two calm down? I'm still trying to blast us out of this volcano!' called a female voice from somewhere else on the ship. Because now I was very confident that I was on a ship. And not just any ship.

I was on TUBS. The spaceship on *Space Blasters*.

I was somehow *in Space Blasters*.

*

I had to be dreaming. That was the only explanation.

But even if I was dreaming, I needed to take control of the situation.

Spaceman Jack and Five-Eyed Frank were still staring at me, so I quickly got to my feet.

'Excuse me,' I said in my most polite voice. 'I am not an it. I am a girl. A human girl,' I clarified, looking at Five-Eyed Frank. 'A human girl named Suzie Wen.'

'We are blasting off in ten, nine, eight, seven . . .' cried the voice from the front.

I looked up and knew from the curly black hair that it was Captain Jane!

'Whatever your name is,' said Spaceman Jack, 'we need to get you in a space chair or else you are going to go **SPLAT** on the ceiling!'

'I just told you my name,' I grumbled, but I followed him to a chair secured to the floor and strapped myself in.

'Six, five, four . . .'

'I SEE LAVA!' screamed Five-Eyed Frank.

'Lava has been outside the window the whole time,' said Spaceman Jack, buckling himself in a space chair next to me. 'Nothing to worry about there, buddy.'

FUN FACT!

Lava is one of the hottest things on Earth and can reach temperatures of over 1,000 degrees Fahrenheit!

'I knew parking inside a volcano was a bad idea!' groaned

29

Five-Eyed Frank as he also climbed into a space chair.

'It was a brilliant idea,' said Spaceman Jack. 'Where else were we going to hide the ship?'

'DANGER! DANGER! RISK OF OVERHEATING!' a mechanical voice echoed all around us. The voice of TUBS!

'BLAST OFF!' yelled Captain Jane and then I was very glad that Spaceman Jack had

insisted I strap into a space chair because with a **ZOOOOM** I was flung back against it, and then we zoomed so fast I could feel my brain bouncing around inside my head.

'Hold on tight, Suzie the Spy!' said Spaceman Jack cheerfully.

'I'm not a spy!'

'That is exactly what a spy would say,' muttered Five-Eyed Frank.

'I'm a SCIENTIST!' I declared. 'And an inventor!'

'Well, that's useful,' said Spaceman Jack. 'We could use a scientist on ship.'

'I still think she's a spy.' All of Five-Eyed Frank's eyes glared at me as the spaceship levelled out and I felt my stomach return to its normal place in my body instead of somewhere in my throat.

'You think everyone is a spy,' said the voice of Captain Jane. And this time it was much closer. She'd left her chair and was now standing next to me. 'But I'll admit . . . I am very curious how a human girl named Suzie ended up on our ship.'

'There aren't even any humans in this solar system,' said Spaceman Jack. 'Or if there are, we haven't seen them.'

'You are a long way from home,' said

Captain Jane.

I stared at them both. 'And *you* live in my TV!'

Captain Jane and Spaceman Jack stared at me for a moment and then burst out laughing. 'We live here on TUBS. Except when we aren't on missions, and then we live on Earth.'

'Well . . . did you know that your adventures are streamed on TV?' I suddenly wondered if this meant that I was on TV too. Could anyone at home see me?

'Who would want to watch us?' scoffed Captain Jane.

'A better question is, who wouldn't?' said Spaceman Jack, admiring his reflection in a window and giving himself a wink.

'Time works differently in space too,' said Captain Jane. 'We haven't been back to Earth in a very long time for us, but not much time has passed at all down there.'

I rubbed my eyes. 'I still think I might be dreaming.'

Five-Eyed Frank reached out with one of his long green arms and pinched me.

'Ow!' I said, rubbing my arm. 'That hurt!'

'Well, now you know you aren't dreaming! Easiest way to tell. What isn't as easy to tell is if you really are a human. Or an alien in disguise!'

I stared at him. 'But aren't you an alien?'

'Yes, of course,' said Five-Eyed Frank patiently. 'But *I'm* not an evil alien. I'm a friendly alien. Everyone knows that. But an alien wearing a human suit . . . those are almost always evil.'

'I'm not an alien wearing a human suit! I'm a human in . . . well, in human clothes!' This was the most ridiculous conversation I'd ever had, and that included trying to convince my po-po that some people actually paid money to swim with sharks. She refused to believe it.

'We probably should do something about your clothes, actually,' said Captain Jane. 'If you are going to be on the ship, you should have the proper protective gear. You need a spacesuit.'

'Wait!' exclaimed Five-Eyed Frank in a panic. 'We have to test her to make SURE she is a human before we let her stay.'

Captain Jane sighed. 'Frank,' she said. 'I think she really is a human girl.'

'We've been tricked before,' said Spaceman Jack. 'I agree with Frank. Better to be safe than sorry.'

'That was ONE time,' said Captain Jane. 'And it was a very good human suit. And a very clever alien. You can't blame me!'

'This could be a very clever alien,' said Five-Eyed Frank suspiciously. 'Wearing a high-quality human suit.'

'I really am a human!' I burst out. 'I don't know how else to prove it.'

'I do!' said Five-Eyed Frank, all of his eyes darting around in excitement. 'Stay here! I'll be right back!' He jumped out of his space seat and scurried off.

'Don't worry,' said Captain Jane. 'He's harmless.' She frowned. 'But I still don't know how you got on my ship.'

I thought carefully about how I actually might have ended up on TUBS. 'I think one of my inventions went wrong, and I accidentally beamed myself up here.'

'Ah,' said Captain Jane nodding. 'That is very possible. The question is, how do we beam you back?'

I looked out of the window at all the stars flying by. I suddenly felt very, very far from home.

CHAPTER 4

THE ALIEN
TEST

Before I could think too much more about
how far I was from home, Five-Eyed
Frank strode back into the room carrying
a purple box and marched right up to
me, so close that our noses were almost
touching. I felt like I was in a staring
contest that I was destined to lose. At
least mathematically, since he had five
eyes to my two.

As if he had read my mind, Five-Eyed
Frank stared unblinkingly at me with all of

his eyes. 'So, *Suzie* . . . if that really is your name . . .'

'It is!'

'There is only ONE way to figure out if you really are human.' He slammed the box down in front of me and waited expectantly.

'Do you want me to open the box?' I said, tentatively poking at it.

Frank sighed dramatically and then turned the box upside down. A stuffed rabbit, a top hat and a deck of playing cards fell out of it. 'Show me a magic trick!' he demanded.

I frowned. 'I don't know any magic tricks.'

'*Aha!*' the alien declared triumphantly. He clapped his hands together in delight. 'I've got you, you imposter. Humans *love* magic. Everyone in the universe knows that.'

'I do too. I mean . . . I like magic. I just don't know any magic tricks.'

Five-Eyed Frank looked over at Spaceman Jack and Captain Jane. 'Well, that proves it then. She's an imposter. A fake. There is zero per cent chance that this being is a *human* being. I say we release her from the spaceship. Right now.'

Spaceman Jack let out a chuckle. 'Don't be so silly, Frank. And stop giving Suzie such a hard time. You know I don't know any magic tricks either. You were just complaining about it the other day.'

Five-Eyed Frank let out a huff. 'It's no secret that it was deeply disappointing for me that you did not know any magic tricks. But I know you well enough to know you aren't like most humans, so I gave you a pass.'

'Maybe there's another test we can do,' said Spaceman Jack, turning his gaze towards me. 'Why don't you tell us a joke?' He winked at me, like he was on my side. But if he really was on my side he would simply tell Five-Eyed Frank that I *obviously* was a human.

Five-Eyed Frank clapped his hands together. 'Yes! Brilliant! That is a great idea,' he said as he put the items back in the purple box and turned back to me. 'If you don't know any magic, you definitely will know a joke. Humans love jokes almost as much as they love magic.'

'Umm . . .' I said, wracking my brain. Why couldn't I think of a single joke? And what if not knowing one made Spaceman Jack and Captain Jane think I wasn't human? I wished my best friend Bonnie was here. Bonnie knows loads of jokes. She would be able to come up with at least one.

'Well?' said Five-Eyed Frank.

I desperately tried to remember the last joke I'd heard. It probably would have been from Bonnie. When I went over to her house to say bye, her little brother had been there and he'd demanded we entertain him (much like Five-Eyed Frank, now that I thought about it). And Bonnie had told him a knock-knock joke! That was it! I cleared my throat. 'Knock-knock!'

Five eyes stared at me blankly. 'What?'

Captain Jane sighed. 'Frank, you have to say *who's there.*'

'Ohh! A knock-knock joke! I've heard of these!' Five-Eyed Frank's eyes lit up. Then he seemed to remember he didn't trust me and glared at me again. 'Who's there?' he said, very seriously.

'Cows say,' I said, trying not to grin. It really was a good joke.

Five-Eyed Frank frowned. 'Cows don't talk.'

'You have to say *cows say who,*' explained Spaceman Jack. 'That's how knock-knock jokes work.'

'All right,' said Five-Eyed Frank suspiciously. 'Cows say who?'

'Cows don't say who, they say MOOOOO!' I declared. I really gave it my best moo too, like a real cow. I wished Bonnie was there to hear it, she would have loved it.

Five-Eyed Frank's frown deepened. 'I don't get it.'

I shrugged. 'Probably because you're an alien. If you were a human, you'd definitely get it.'

Five-Eyed-Frank looked over at Spaceman Jack. 'Did you think the joke was funny?'

'Erm . . . not exactly, but there is no denying it was a joke,' said Spaceman Jack. 'No offence, Suzie.'

'I thought jokes were supposed to be funny,' said Five-Eyed Frank.

'Hey, it wasn't that bad of a joke,' I said. 'And my cow impression was pretty funny.'

'I wouldn't know, I've never met a cow,' said Five-Eyed Frank. 'We don't have any cows in outer space.'

I cleared my throat and did my very best

moo. This one was even better than the last.

Five-Eyed Frank burst out laughing. 'That *is* funny.'

'So do you believe me now?'

Five-Eyed Frank stared hard at me, and then nodded. 'Yes! You really are a human. Palm five!' He held out his hand to me.

'Do you mean "high five"?'

'No, I mean palm five. I want us to touch palms while holding up five fingers, at an exactly medium height.'

'Got it. Palm five!' I gave Five-Eyed Frank a high five and grinned at him. I'd successfully proven I was not an alien. That was one less thing to worry about!

FUN JOKES!

What music do aliens listen to?
Nep-tunes!

Why do stars go to school?
To get brighter!

Why didn't the moon want dinner?
It was too full!

CHAPTER 5

PLANET CHEDDAR

'This doesn't mean we are friends or anything like that,' said Five-Eyed Frank, quickly putting his hands behind his back like he was already regretting giving me a palm five. 'All it proves is that you are human.'

'Indeed she is,' said Captain Jane, giving me a wide smile. 'Now that is settled, I'm going to take a nap. It has been a very exciting and exhausting morning. Spaceman Jack, you're in charge. Suzie, if you need anything, just come wake me up. I'll be in the crew's quarters right over there.' She pointed to a room off to the side.

'What about the ship?' I said. 'Who is flying it if you are napping?'

'Oh, don't worry about that. TUBS basically flies itself, except when it comes to take-off and landing. I've put it on autopilot to follow a standard route. We're headed to Planet Mondo, and we won't be there for a while.'

'Is Planet Mondo near Planet Earth?' I said hopefully.

'Of course not! It isn't even in the same solar system! We are light years away from Earth,' said Five-Eyed Frank.

'Oh.'

'Don't worry, Suzie. We'll figure out how to get you home,' said Captain Jane kindly.

Then she yawned. 'I'll be much better at coming up with a plan after I've had a little sleep.'

'Have a good nap,' I said, even though what I really wanted to say was 'TAKE ME HOME RIGHT NOW'. But part of me was a tiny bit excited to get to spend more time on the ship. After all, it wasn't every day that I got to go to space!

After Captain Jane disappeared, me, Five-Eyed Frank and Spaceman Jack sat in silence for a moment. Then there was a small squeak – a birdlike chirp – right above my head. I looked up and gasped. Because floating above me was a three-headed lizard. 'Whoa! What is that?'

'This right here is Tommy, and he goes everywhere the Space Blasters go,' said Spaceman Jack.

'Oh!' I suddenly remembered seeing Three-Headed Tommy on a *Space Blasters* episode. Spaceman Jack had saved him when he was a tiny lizard caught on a burning planet, and ever since then Tommy had been loyal to Spaceman Jack.

One of the lizard heads turned to me and stuck its tongue out. The other head had its eyes closed, and the third one was yawning.

'Nice to meet you, Tommy,' I said. The head closest to me let out another friendly chirp in reply, and then Tommy flew even closer and stuck out one of his tongues and licked my face. I giggled and held out my hand. Tommy landed on it and tilted all three of his heads to the side inquisitively. He chirped again.

'Aw, that means he likes you!' said

Spaceman Jack. 'He's a good three-headed lizard. The best friend a man can have.'

'Isn't that what people say about dogs?' I said, tentatively petting one of Tommy's heads.

'Who would want a dog when you could have Tommy?' said Spaceman Jack.

'Good point!' I said, smiling at Tommy. 'A three-headed lizard is way cooler!'

'The lizard is a terrible judge of character,' sniffed Five-Eyed Frank. 'Clearly he'll just trust *anybody*.'

'Hey! Didn't I just prove to you that I am a human?'

'That doesn't mean anything about your *character*,' said Five-Eyed Frank. 'It just means you are a tailess primate with bipedalism.'

'What is bipedalism?' I spoke slowly,

trying to pronounce the word right.

'It means you have two feet that you can walk upright on. Obviously.' Five-Eyed Frank rolled all five of his eyes.

'Be nice, Frank,' said Spaceman Jack.

'All I'm saying is that a test of character isn't as easy as a test to prove she's human. No matter how much the lizard likes her.'

I grinned at Tommy. At least *somebody* on this ship liked me.

'Well, I like her too,' said Spaceman Jack. I puffed up with pride, even as Five-Eyed Frank's scowl deepened. 'Oh, cheer up, Frank,' Spaceman Jack went on. 'Now we've got an extra player for space checkers! You're always saying how bored you are just playing me.'

'Oh! That is cheering,' said Five-Eyed

Frank. 'We should play right now.' He smiled broadly. 'I am excellent at space checkers.'

'What is space checkers?' I said.

'You don't know very much, do you?' said Five-Eyed Frank. 'Even for a human.'

I bristled. 'I know lots of stuff. And it is OK not to know things. Nobody is born knowing everything.'

'Untrue,' said Five-Eyed Frank. 'Knowledge worms from Planet Zorg are born knowing everything.'

'Well, I'm not a knowledge worm.'

'A shame. I've always wanted to meet a knowledge worm.'

'If she was a knowledge worm, she'd probably beat you at space checkers,' said

Spaceman Jack. 'So, probably best that she's just a human girl.' Then he turned to me. 'It's like regular checkers, except with four boards and the pieces float,' he said. 'You'll get the hang of it.'

*

Four games later, and I had *not* got the hang of it.

'But how come this red one can leapfrog over four and then go diagonal?' I said. 'That isn't in the rules.'

'Maybe not in Earth checkers, but we're in space, remember?' said Five-Eyed Frank.

'It's hard to forget,' I said, glancing out of the window at the stars flying by. Then I did a double take. I didn't see any stars. Instead I saw a big yellow planet. One that was alarmingly close! 'Um. I'm sure you both know way more about flying a spaceship than me, but it looks like we are about to crash into that planet?'

Five-Eyed Frank laughed. 'Don't be ridiculous! We're on a standard flight path like Captain Jane said.'

The planet in the window grew bigger and bigger as we torpedoed straight towards it.

'Well, maybe something is wrong with TUBS. Because we are definitely about to crash into a big yellow planet covered in holes.'

'Nope. Not possible,' said Spaceman Jack. 'TUBS never makes a mistake.'

'I really think we should wake up Captain Jane!' I said. Without waiting for permission, I ran in the direction of the crew's quarters. 'Captain Jane!' I cried. 'We need you!'

Seconds later she stumbled out of her room, eyes wide. 'What's the emergency?'

'Look!' I said, pointing out of the window. 'We're about to crash!'

'Flying macaroni!' she said. 'You're right!'

She hit a button on the wall. 'TUBS! Avert course collision!' And then she raced to the captain's seat. 'Everybody, get in your space chairs, NOW!'

I didn't waste any time. I jumped into the nearest space chair and strapped myself in.

Captain Jane pulled on the ship's controls.

'We're too close!' she cried. 'We're getting sucked in by the planet's gravitational pull! We'll have to make a crash landing!' The ship was speeding up, and veering wildly from side to side, and my stomach was sloshing around with it.

Spaceman Jack scratched his head. 'But that planet shouldn't *be* there. This is a clear route!'

'I don't know why it is there either,' said Captain Jane. 'But the important thing is, it *is* there! Now hold on to your space boots, this is going to be a bumpy ride!'

I glanced down at my watermelon socks. I didn't even have shoes

FUN FACT!

Gravity keeps the Earth's moon close to Earth. If it weren't for gravity, our moon would float away!

to hold on to, never mind space boots!

'Hey, Suzie,' said Five-Eyed Frank from the chair across from me. I looked up. He gave me a big, toothy smile that I think was meant to be nice but was actually pretty terrifying. 'You've convinced me. You're definitely human.'

I grinned back at him, even as I felt my palms getting more and more sweaty.

'And you are a hero too!' said Spaceman Jack. 'Or you will be if we survive this.'

'*If* we survive?' I squeaked.

'Don't worry!' said Captain Jane. 'We always do!'

'There's a first time for everything,' said Five-Eyed Frank. 'But if I'm going to die, I'm going down bravely! With the ship! Singing!' He began to sing, but in a serious, almost sad, way.

Spaceman Jack joined him and they began to harmonise.

I'd definitely never heard Spaceman Jack sing on the show before. They were way stranger in real life!

'*And with my face in the starrrrs, they will know where we arrree!*' he trilled.

'No, no,' said Five-Eyed Frank. 'Those aren't the lyrics. It's "*we've come so faaaaar, just look where we arrrre.*"'

There was a tremendous **THUD** and then everything, even Five-Eyed Frank and Spaceman Jack, went quiet.

'Exactly, look where we are!' said Captain Jane triumphantly. 'We made it! And all in one piece!'

There was a loud *crack* and the whole spaceship shuddered.

A mechanical voice spoke over the speakers. **'Damage alert! Damage alert! Repair needed. TUBS is shutting down. Repeat – TUBS is shutting down.'**

I gulped. Uh-oh. Now I was never going to get home! 'Where have we landed?' I said, leaning my head over to look out of the window. A strong stench hit my nose. 'And what is that *smell*?'

'Welcome to Planet Cheddar,' said

Spaceman Jack, holding his nose. 'We've never landed here before, we've only flown over it. And now I realise why.'

'I'm glad I have five eyes and not five noses,' said Five-Eyed Frank. 'Yuck!'

'TUBS? Report the damage,' said Captain Jane. 'TUBS?'

I cleared my throat. 'I think it said it was shutting down.'

'But TUBS never shuts down!' said Five-Eyed Frank in a panic.

'Everyone stay calm,' said Captain Jane. 'All we need to do is go outside the ship and see what the damage is.'

'GO OUTSIDE THE SHIP?' wailed Five-Eyed Frank. 'ON A NEW PLANET?'

'Frank, you know nobody is going to make you go outside unless you want to,' said Captain Jane patiently. 'You can stay in the ship, like you usually do.'

'The human girl can stay with you,' added Spaceman Jack.

'No way!' Five-Eyed Frank and I exclaimed at the same time.

'No offence,' I added. 'I just want to explore a new planet! This is my first time being anywhere other than Earth.' Then I frowned. 'Why don't you want me to stay with you?'

'Haven't you ever heard of stranger danger?' said Five-Eyed Frank. 'I just met you!'

'Yeah, and you tested me to make sure I'm a human.'

'Exactly! Everyone knows humans are the most untrustworthy beings in all the universe.'

'Well, I'm a very trustworthy human,' I said.

'I'll believe it when I see it,' said Five-Eyed Frank, wiggling his eyes at me. 'Remember, just because you're a human it doesn't tell us anything about your character.'

'I'll prove how trustworthy I am! I bet I can figure out what's wrong with the spaceship.'

'Really?' said Captain Jane. 'But you don't know anything about TUBS.'

I nodded with more confidence than I felt. 'Fixing things is my speciality!' They didn't need to know that sometimes the things I fixed had a tendency to explode. 'I'm sure I can figure it out!'

'Well, thank the moons for that,' said Spaceman Jack. 'I'm a terrible mechanic. Hate it when the oil gets in my hair.'

Captain Jane studied me for a moment.

'I think we have a spacesuit that we used for a monkey once that might fit you.'

'A monkey?'

'Don't take it personally, you are just much smaller than our usual crew. And you definitely can't go outside without a spacesuit.'

'I miss that monkey,' said Spaceman Jack fondly. 'Good old Gertie.'

'What happened to her?' I really didn't want to put on a spacesuit that a monkey had died in.

'She got too old for space adventures, so she retired. The funny thing is, she didn't want to go back to Earth! She chose a tropical planet in the Zadar galaxy. Last we checked, she was sleeping on the beach and drinking from coconuts so big she could swim in them.'

'Sounds like a good life,' I said.

'Why couldn't we have crash-landed on
that planet?' groaned Five-Eyed Frank.

'Nobody chooses where they crash-land,'
said Spaceman Jack. 'All you can do is hope
for the best and enjoy the ride.' He stroked
his chin. 'That's a good one. I should write
it down.'

I remembered that on the show, Spaceman Jack frequently said sayings that he found inspiring and wise. I wondered how much of what actually happened on the spaceship ended up on the TV show. Five-Eyed Frank sure seemed friendlier on the episodes I'd seen. But now that I thought about it, I'd never seen him interact with any other humans or aliens other than the Space Blasters crew. Maybe he just didn't like strangers.

'We aren't on a tropical planet, we're on a smelly cheese one, and there's nothing we can do about it until we fix TUBS,' said Captain Jane. 'Now come on. The faster we get out there the faster we can leave.'

*

Luckily Gertrude's suit did fit me. And if it smelled like a monkey, I couldn't tell because all I could smell was stinky cheese.

Captain Jane put the space helmet on my head. 'Now remember,' she said. 'Keep your helmet on at all times. Not only because you need to be able to breathe, but also, if we can smell the stinky cheese through the walls of TUBS, imagine how awful it will be out there with nothing to protect your nose.'

I nodded. I couldn't believe that I was about to go explore another planet!

Sure, it was a planet that looked and smelled like cheese, but still. I was doing the kind of things that real-life scientists did!

We went into the exit chamber. 'One other thing,' said Captain Jane. 'The gravity here will be different from what you are used to. It is a low-gravity planet, so you will feel lighter and jump higher – but don't worry, you won't float off into space!'

She pressed a button and a door popped open and a slide shot out from the side of TUBS. 'Down we go.' She leaped out the door, feet first.

'You go next,' said Spaceman Jack. 'I'll be right behind you!' I walked over to the open door and gulped. 'Well, here goes!'

The slide was *very* slick. I slid down like a slippery fish covered in butter. Before I knew it, I whooshed off the end and landed feet first.

This was it, my first step on a new planet. One small step for me, Suzie Wen, one giant step for kids everywhere!

Then I realised my feet were stuck.

'I thought you said this planet had low gravity!' I cried out to Captain Jane, who was in front of me trying to yank her own foot out of the mushy ground.

'I didn't realise the ground would be so squishy!' she said. Then she looked behind me and panic filled her eyes.

'Quick! Move out of the way! Spaceman Jack is coming down – he's going to crash right into you!'

With one final yank on my borrowed space boots, I heaved my foot out of the squishy yellow ground and dodged out of the way just in time.

Moments later, Spaceman Jack flew off the slide. As he exited, he grinned and waved, like he was expecting a camera crew and cheering crowds. But as he landed, his feet sank into the cheese floor, and then he staggered forward and sank to his knees. 'Ugh. I'm never going to get the smell out of my spacesuit!'

'Let's fix TUBS and get out of here,' said Captain Jane, carefully picking her way across the squishy ground. 'I think the damage is on the left side of the ship.'

She frowned. 'I still don't know what went wrong. TUBS was on the right route. This planet popped up out of nowhere!'

'That's strange,' I said. 'So if the spaceship was in the right place that means the PLANET was in the wrong place! Maybe while we are here we can figure out why the planet is out of orbit and isn't where it's supposed to be?'

'An excellent idea,' said Captain Jane.

I took another step, and suddenly the ground beneath my feet opened up and swallowed me whole.

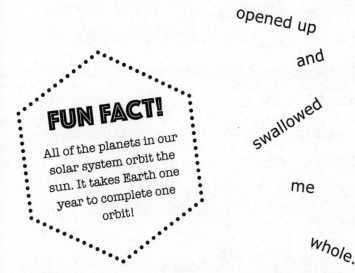

FUN FACT!

All of the planets in our solar system orbit the sun. It takes Earth one year to complete one orbit!

I was so surprised I didn't even scream.
I tumbled down the hole, trying to grab on
to the sides to slow myself down, but it was
no use.

Stay calm, stay calm, I told myself as
it grew darker and darker all around me
and the smell of cheese grew stronger and
stronger.

Suddenly I landed with a thump on
something soft.

Soft and *moving.*

I gulped. I'd found whatever life forms
lived on Planet Cheddar . . .

CHAPTER 6

BABBITS

There was a scurrying and a scratching sound. And then two huge luminous-green eyes stared up at me.

I scuttled back, but couldn't go far before I was stuck against a wall of smelly cheese.

Another pair of eyes appeared, and then another, and another, until I was surrounded by glowing green eyes.

There was a squeak, and another, louder and louder until all the creatures around me were squeaking and . . . hopping?

I squinted in the dim light. Were these rabbits?

'HOLD ON, SUZIE, I'M COMING DOWN!' thundered a voice from above, and moments later Spaceman Jack came abseiling down the tunnel, with a torch on his head. As the light lit up the tunnel, the creatures screeched and I saw that they *were* rabbits.

If rabbits were the size of dogs and had glowing green eyes and blue fur.

'Watch out!' cried Spaceman Jack, and then he landed in a crouch beside me. He held out his hands in a peaceful manner. 'Hello! We come in peace!'

The rabbits, or whatever they were, stared at us with their huge eyes.

Now that there was more light, I saw that only four of the creatures were actually awake. But there was a whole pile of them, maybe hundreds, that I'd landed on. And all of those were seemingly asleep, their eyes closed and little noses twitching with gentle snores.

One of the four blue rabbit creatures that *was* awake let out a series of high-pitched squeaks. Spaceman Jack winced at the noise. 'Hold on, hold on, let me turn on my language transmitter.' He pressed a button on the side of his suit.

'You've got one too,' he said to me, nodding. I looked down at the arm of my spacesuit and frowned. There were tons of different buttons! I didn't want to accidentally press the wrong one and catapult myself somewhere (although that would actually be useful for getting out of this alien-rabbit den), or open up my space helmet!

'It's the green one shaped like an ear,' said Spaceman Jack. 'But be careful not to press the red one shaped like a flame next to it.'

I very carefully pressed the green button, and all of a sudden the squeaking sounds turned into words! English words!

My jaw dropped.

'Hello! Hello! Humans! We have not met humans before! Why are you here?'

'Our ship crash-landed,' said Spaceman Jack. He pressed another button on his suit and a scanner popped out of his shoulder and cast a red light on the strange blue rabbits.

The creatures squeaked indignantly and shut their eyes.

The scanner seemed to be cataloguing them, and then a little bell went off.

'*BABBIT,*' said a robotic voice. 'A friendly race of lagomorphs* who live on Planet Cheddar. Non-aggressive unless startled. Very strong back legs.'

'Surely shining a laser into their eyes might startle them!' I said, stepping forward to shield the babbits.

FUN FACT!

*a lagomorph is the family of animals that rabbits and hares belong to – and apparently babbits!

The laser went over me. 'Human girl. Wearing a spacesuit designed for a monkey.'

I gaped. 'You made me do those tests when you had this thing the whole time!'

Spaceman Jack shrugged. 'I forgot about it. Useful, though.' He nodded to himself and then literally patted himself on the back.

'Back to the babbits,' I said, turning to the blue creatures. 'I'm sorry if we woke you when we . . . erm, fell on you.'

The one I had decided was the leader, or at least was the most outspoken, shook its head. 'No! No! Not sleeping! This is not our hibernation time! We should be awake! We should be burrowing! Digging! Preparing for the cold season! Lots of work to do! But we are all falling asleep, and now cannot wake up! Look!'

The babbit wound up its back leg and

directed a powerful kick to the sleeping babbit behind it. I winced, but the babbit merely rolled over and continued snoring.

'Nothing will wake them! We are the only ones awake on the entire planet! And we would have fallen asleep too – but then you fell on us!'

'Just in time!' chirped another babbit.

'Saved us from the sleep!' said another.

I frowned. 'What do you mean, you are all falling asleep?'

'We dig as a group,' the head babbit explained. 'To prepare for hibernation season. Under here we are warm and safe and have plenty of cheese to eat. And then we emerge fat and happy for hopping season!'

'What is hopping season?'

'The season for hopping! We hop all over

the planet to make sure that the ground is ready for digging in the cold season.'

'So you spend one season preparing for the other?'

'Exactly! And every season we eat the cheese.'

'Sounds like a good life,' said Spaceman Jack appreciatively. 'Eating cheese, sleeping, digging. I think I would make a good babbit.'

'But we should not be sleeping now!' The babbit's eyes grew even wider. 'Something has happened. What if I cannot wake them?'

'Don't worry,' I said, trying to sound confident. 'We will help you. We're here to figure out why your planet is out of orbit, and why everyone is sleeping!'

'I thought you said you crash-landed

here,' said another babbit, sounding slightly
suspicious.

'Well, we did,' I said. 'But now that we're
here, we can help!' I turned to Spaceman
Jack. 'Right, Spaceman Jack?'

He groaned. 'We can't help every alien
we come across in the galaxy.'

'Yes, we can! Isn't that one of the Space
Blasters' mottos?' I said, putting my
hands on my hips. 'That is what saving the

universe means! Helping
people!'

'Shootin' stars, I
think I've been told,'
said Spaceman Jack.
'You're right, small
space girl! We should
help these babbits!'

CHAPTER 7

THE SCIENTIFIC METHOD

'This sounds like the perfect opportunity to apply the scientific method!' I declared.

'What in the name of jumping Jupiter is the scientific method?' said Spaceman Jack, and I could have sworn he went to scratch his head before he remembered he was wearing a space helmet.

I cleared my throat. 'The scientific method is how you figure things out! There are seven steps. Observe. Question. Hypothesise. Experiment. Analyse. Conclude. Report!'

THE SCIENTIFIC METHOD

Step one: Observe what is happening.

Step two: Figure out the question you are trying to answer. Or a problem you are trying to solve.

Step three: Hypothesise — a fancy way of saying take all the information you have and guess what the answer is, based on your observations.

Step four: Experiment — my favourite! Test out your hypothesis to see if it is correct.

Step five: Analyse — look at all of the results from your experiment.

Step six: Conclude — decide what your results are telling you and try to come up with an answer, and see if your hypothesis (or guess) was correct.

Step seven: Report — write it down so you can share your results with the world!

Congratulations, you have run a successful experiment!

Spaceman Jack cleared his throat. 'Exactly how long is this going to take? We can't stay on Planet Cheddar forever, you know.'

I grinned. 'Lucky for you, we've already observed! Here is what we know so far.' I began to pace in the small hole, careful not to step on any of the sleeping babbits.

The babbits are sleeping when they shouldn't be. The planet is out of orbit.

I looked up. 'Now with those observations, it is time to come up with a question.' I stopped walking and stared at the babbits. 'Hmm . . . I think our question is *why* are the babbits asleep?'

'I sure don't know,' said Spaceman Jack. 'I don't have a single guess.'

'Well, maybe we need more information.'
I looked at the babbits. 'I need to ask you
a few more questions. But can we go back
above ground?'

The biggest babbit nodded. 'Climb on my
back! I'll hop you right out of here.'

Spaceman Jack gulped. 'I think I'll climb
back up myself, using my rope.' He pressed
another button on his suit and a rope shot
out and anchored itself to the top of the
hole. 'Are you all right going on the babbit?'
he said to me.

'Are you kidding? It sounds amazing!' I
beamed at the babbit. 'Thanks!'

'Thank you for helping us!'

'See you space bunnies up there!' said
Spaceman Jack, and he started to climb up
the cheesy walls.

'Ready?' said the babbit.

I carefully climbed on the babbit's back and held on to its ears. 'Ready!'

With one giant bound, the babbit hopped straight out of the cheese tunnel and back above ground.

The sky was a dark purple, and there were millions of stars out. I hadn't noticed when we'd landed because I'd been so distracted by the cheese smell, and the whole crash-landing situation, but now that I was taking a moment to look around I couldn't believe how beautiful it was!

It was like we were on a huge ball of cheese, floating in a big bowl of sparkling purple jam.

'Wow!' I said, staring up at the sky.

'Yes, our stars are very beautiful,' said the babbit. Then it frowned. 'But where is our moon?'

I frowned. 'Your moon?'

'Yes! We have a wonderful big moon. We should be able to see it!'

'That sounds like useful information,' I said, and I wrote it down in my notebook

'There you are!' said a voice from behind me. I turned round to see Captain Jane hurrying over. 'What took you so long to get out of that hole?' Then she spotted the babbit and grinned. 'A babbit! I've always wanted to see one!'

The babbit puffed up with pride. 'Hello, new human! This small human is helping us!'

I quickly told Captain Jane everything that we'd learned. 'So now I am doing the scientific method so we can figure out what is going on.'

'I can't argue with the scientific method,'

said Captain Jane. 'And it does sound like the babbits need our help.' She frowned. 'And that is rather alarming about the moon going missing. I've never heard of anything like that happening.'

'Highly unusual,' said the babbit, hopping up and down.

There was a loud grunt next to us and Spaceman Jack pulled himself up out of the tunnel. 'I should have gone with the babbit! Climbing out of that thing was way harder than jumping down into it!'

Captain Jane laughed. 'Yes, that is usually the case.'

I looked at the babbit. 'Was there anyone else awake? Did anyone actually *see* the moon disappear? I think I need more information before I can make a hypothesis.'

'I did!' squeaked a new voice.

I glanced around. Where had that come from?

'Down here!'

A small babbit head suddenly poked out of a pocket in the big babbit's fur, like a kangaroo! It was a baby babbit!

'Oh! Hello there!' I held out my hand and the baby babbit hopped into my palm.

'I'm always the last one down in the digging tunnel because I'm the smallest,' explained the baby babbit. 'So I was up here by myself, about to jump in, when I saw it.'

The baby babbit's eyes grew huge as she stared up at the sky. 'The moon was stolen right out of the sky!'

Spaceman Jack sighed. 'So much for the big reveal. It isn't possible.'

'You don't know that,' I said.

'I promise!' squeaked the babbit. 'It was there one minute, and then the sky got really cloudy, with big purple clouds, and the next minute ZoOoOM! The moon and the clouds went that way!' it pointed with its ears.

'Hold on,' I said. 'I need to write all this down!'

I wrote down everything we knew.

BABBITS ASLEEP
PLANET OUT OF ORBIT
MOVING MOON

Hmm. I wondered if the planet's orbit and their moon were connected . . . Could the planet be out of orbit because of the missing moon?

I looked up. 'I think I have a hypothesis.' I took a deep breath. 'Something moved the moon, and that knocked the planet out of orbit.'

'And the sleeping babbits?' said Spaceman Jack.

'That's the part I can't connect,' I admitted. 'We need more information. We have to observe more.' I looked up at

Captain Jane. 'Can we . . . chase a moon?'

A thoughtful expression crossed her face. 'We can try. We'll go in the same direction it went. It can't have gone too far, it's a moon, after all.'

'Hold on,' said Spaceman Jack. 'We're going to take the word of a baby babbit and go on a wild goose chase?'

'More like a wild moon chase,' I said. I lifted the baby babbit up so I was looking right into its huge eyes. 'We'll figure out what is happening, and we'll wake up the rest of the babbits. I promise.'

'Oh, now you've done it,' groaned Spaceman Jack. 'If we promise, we'll have to come back.'

'Of course we have to come back!' I said. 'We're helping them! But first we have to go chase that moon.'

'You're forgetting a key detail,' said Spaceman Jack. 'TUBS is damaged, remember? We have to repair the ship first.'

Captain Jane grinned. 'You're in luck. I managed to fix it while you two were down in that cheese tunnel. One of the side panels fell off during landing and a wire short-circuited, but it's good to go now!'

I gently put the baby babbit back in the big babbit's pouch.

'Keep an eye out for anything else suspicious,' I said. 'And thank you for welcoming us to your planet.'

FUN FACT!
Did you know that the planet Jupiter has seventy nine moons?

'You can come back any time you like, small human,' said the big babbit, wrinkling its nose at me.

I gave it a salute, and then followed
Spaceman Jack and Captain Jane back on
to the ship.

It was time to chase a moon.

CHAPTER 8

WELCOME TO
THE CREW

'Well, Suzie,' said Captain Jane once we were back on the ship. 'It looks like you are now officially part of the Space Blasters crew.'

'Really?' I couldn't believe it!

'What? When did that happen? Why wasn't I consulted?' wailed Five-Eyed Frank.

'She put on a spacesuit and bravely offered to help others. If that doesn't make her part of the Space Blasters crew, I don't know what does,' said Captain Jane, giving me a huge smile. 'We'll celebrate with a space feast tonight.'

'I didn't get a welcome space feast!' sputtered Five-Eyed Frank.

'That is because you don't eat human food,' said Spaceman Jack. 'You eat nails.'

'Well. A feast would still have been nice,' sulked Five-Eyed Frank.

'You can share my feast,' I said. 'It can be for both of us.'

'Can it be fifty-five per cent my feast and forty-five per cent your feast?' Five-Eyed Frank's eyes watched me carefully.

'Sure,' I said. Because I was so excited to officially be part of the Space Blasters crew, I was more than happy to share.

'I think I should get at least five per cent

of the feast,' said Spaceman Jack. 'I wanted
to help the babbits too, you know.'

Captain Jane rolled her eyes. 'Fine. It's a
feast for all of us. Are you happy now?'

'Can I have a cake?' said Five-Eyed Frank.

'You can't even eat cake!'

'I know. But I like to look at one.'

'I'll see what we have in the kitchen,' said
Captain Jane. 'But first, we have to take off.'

'So how are we going to track this

moon?' said Spaceman Jack as we settled into our space chairs. It already felt normal to me, and I knew how to strap myself in and everything. I looked out of the window and saw the babbits waving their ears in goodbye. I waved back.

'We'll start by going in the direction the baby babbit pointed in, and I'll do a scan to see if there are any unexpected moons floating around,' said Captain Jane.

'I have a suggestion,' I said. This was my moment to really prove my worth to the crew, and I was ready for it.

'Yes?' said Captain Jane.

'We should also look for any other planets that are out of their usual orbit, right?'

'Hoppin' horn frogs, that's right!' said Spaceman Jack. 'I should have thought of that.'

'An excellent suggestion, Suzie,' said Captain Jane. 'Well done.'

I grinned back at her and settled into my seat, just in time to see Five-Eyed Frank glaring at me with all five of his eyes.

'I could have thought of that,' he said.

Something occurred to me. Was Five-Eyed Frank . . . jealous of me? It seemed impossible that a five-eyed alien who lived on a spaceship was jealous of me, a human girl lost in space who had no idea what she was doing, but he certainly was acting like it. He had always seemed so friendly on the show!

'And blast off!' said Captain Jane. TUBS rumbled to life and shot up into the air, leaving the babbits behind.

My ears popped and I felt my stomach swoop, but a few moments later, we were back up amidst the stars. I turned to Five-Eyed Frank, who was still pouting in his chair. I remembered from the show that he was the one who usually came up with ideas for the crew.

'I bet you have lots of great ideas,' I said.

'I do! I am the ideas machine of the ship,' he said, cheering up for just a moment before frowning again. 'At least I was before you came along.'

'Well, you know what they say. Two

heads are better than one!' I grinned and leaned my head towards him.

'I have five eyes, I don't need two heads,' said Five-Eyed Frank, turning away from me.

I sighed. Oh well. I'd just have to convince Five-Eyed Frank that we were meant to be friends. I always liked a challenge!

'I find that three heads is the best number, myself,' said Spaceman Jack. 'Don't you, Tommy?' He nodded up at the three-headed lizard, who had just floated in from one of the other chambers of the ship.

Tommy gave out a little chirp, and landed on my shoulder. I giggled as he stuck out one of his tongues and licked my face in greeting. 'Hi, friend!' I said.

'He isn't your friend,' Five-Eyed Frank

said, glowering at both of us.

'Not yet,' I said, forcing my voice to be cheerful even as I felt the sting of Five-Eyed Frank's words go all the way down to my toes. 'But I bet by the end of the day we'll be friends for sure.'

I hoped that Five-Eyed Frank knew I wasn't just talking about me and Tommy.

'I like that attitude,' said Spaceman Jack, nodding approvingly.

Five-Eyed Frank made an indignant sputtering sound and closed all of his eyes.

Captain Jane, who had been watching everything carefully, unbuckled her seat and walked over to me. 'Well, Suzie, as the newest member of the crew, do you want to go see the rest of the ship? We should probably show you where everything is.'

'I'd love that!' I said. But then I suddenly

thought about my parents, and I got a lump in my throat. I swallowed and blinked, trying to hold back my emotions. Tommy must have noticed something, because he chirped again and pressed one of his heads against my face. It tickled and made me laugh, despite how homesick I felt. I looked up at Captain Jane. 'But . . . I am going to get back home eventually, right?'

Captain Jane crouched down next to me so we were eye level. 'I will do everything in my power to get you back home. But it might take a little while. And right now you want to help the babbits and sort out this whole missing moon problem, right?'

'Right,' I said. I could go home after that. Surely chasing the moon and solving the mystery of the sleeping babbits couldn't take *that* long. I'd be home before I knew it. And I didn't want to miss out on what was sure to be the BIGGEST adventure of my life! I took a deep breath. 'I definitely want to help.'

'That's the spirit,' said Captain Jane. 'We need you, Suzie. The crew, and the entire universe. Who knows how many other planets are floating out of orbit?'

'I won't let you down,' I said firmly. And then I remembered the Space Blasters' motto. '**FOR THE UNIVERSE!**' I declared, shooting my hand up into the sky like a rocket. I glanced at Five-Eyed Frank, hoping he'd join in, but he kept his eyes determinedly shut. I knew he wasn't sleeping, and for a moment I felt deflated, but then Tommy chirped in agreement and pointed all three of his snouts up in the air in his own version of the Space Blasters'

salute. And that cheered me right up.

'**FOR THE UNIVERSE!**' Spaceman
Jack and Captain Jane cried out. I beamed
at them, and for the first time since I'd
boarded the ship, I truly felt like I was part
of the crew.

My parents would have to understand if
I was gone for a little bit longer. After all,
I was helping to save the entire universe!

CHAPTER 9

SPACE STRAWBERRIES

The heart of the ship was the command centre – which is where the crew spent most of their time.

But the rest of TUBS was almost like a house, except WAY cooler! In the sleeping quarters there were little pods in the walls where we could sleep. When Captain Jane showed me which one would be mine, I climbed in eagerly and lay down. It was like the cosiest bunk bed ever! Then I had a *terrible* thought. 'Wait,' I said. 'Is this where Gertrude the monkey slept?' No offence to Gertrude, but I didn't want to sleep where a monkey had slept! I already had to wear her old spacesuit.

Captain Jane laughed. 'No, we have plenty of sleep pods in case we ever need to bring on more crew members.'

The kitchen was called the canteen, and it was super-duper high-tech. There were no stoves (Captain Jane said it was too dangerous to have an open fire on a spaceship) but there was a giant fridge with plenty of freeze-dried space food, and a fancy microwave to heat everything up.

And behind the canteen was one of the coolest parts of the ship – the mini greenhouse! It wasn't made of glass, like greenhouses on Earth; it was just a small room. Because this one wasn't powered

SPACE MENU

TUBS Special Turkey Sandwich

Space Blastin' Spaghetti

Flying Fish Fingers

Popping Peas

Galaxy's Best Cheesy Chips

Space Salad

Starry Ice Cream

Moon Rock Pie (for Frank ONLY)

by the sun, it was powered by special lights that mimicked sunlight. And that meant they were able to grow fresh food in pots! Carrots, peas, strawberries, chillies, herbs and all kinds of stuff!

'Five-Eyed Frank is an excellent gardener,' said Captain Jane. 'He can show you how he likes to sing to the plants to help them grow.'

I bit my lip. 'Captain Jane, can I ask you something?'

She gave me a warm smile. 'You can always ask the captain something. That is part of my job.'

'I don't think Five-Eyed Frank likes me very much,' I admitted. 'I don't know why. Do you?'

'Oh, don't worry about that. He's suspicious of new people. But he'll warm up eventually. Try not to take it personally.'

I sighed. 'OK.'

'Here, have a space strawberry.' Captain Jane tossed me one of the small strawberries.

Suddenly it hit me that I was eating food that had been grown in OUTER SPACE. It was the best strawberry I'd ever had.

We continued our tour around the ship.
There was a sick bay, which basically was
a doctor's office, bathrooms (I didn't ask
too many questions about where the space
poop went . . .), and even a relaxation and
recreation room! It had a huge screen for
movies, but that also doubled as a 3-D
interactive screen for playing golf or fishing
or lots of different activities that Spaceman
Jack and Captain Jane might want to do
when they missed home. It was almost
exactly like what I had tried to create with
my Super 3-D TV Gizmo!

'Do you miss home?' I asked as she
showed me how to play tennis with
a virtual partner. I didn't tell her that
actually I was terrible at tennis – and
I definitely wasn't interested in playing

virtual golf. Why would you play pretend golf when you could look out at the stars flying by?

Captain Jane looked thoughtful. 'TUBS is my home now,' she said. 'Whenever I go back down to Earth, it feels more like a visit or a holiday.' Then she grinned. 'I don't think I'll ever want to stop having space adventures.'

Finally, Captain Jane took me to the room I was most excited about.

The Gadget Room.

It was FULL of amazing inventions! Special cameras for recording their space missions, helmets for different climates and oxygen levels, all-vision goggles (according to Captain Jane they could be used in the dark, in very bright light, underwater, anywhere!), jet packs, and about a million

other things. I could have stayed in there
forever.

'If we can't find you, I know where you'll
be,' said Captain Jane. 'It's good to have an

inventor on the ship. We always need new gadgets!'

I blushed. 'I wouldn't call myself an inventor.'

Captain Jane raised an eyebrow. 'Why not?'

I picked up a remote that apparently could detect life on any planet and inspected it. 'Well . . . my inventions don't always work out as I thought they would.'

'That's just how life is,' said Captain Jane. 'We all think things are going to be one way, and well, they usually turn out a little bit differently.' She smiled at me. 'You'll learn that quickly on this ship. We've always got to adapt to new situations. But you are already doing great at that. After all, everything here is new to you.'

'But I'm *not* good at adapting,' I said, looking down at the remote. 'I don't like change. My best friend just moved away, and so did my grandparents, and I feel like my whole life is different and I don't know what to do about it.'

I let out a big sigh. It felt good to tell her how I was feeling. I hadn't told anyone, and it had all been bottling up inside of me.

Captain Jane nodded. 'I understand that. Change can be hard sometimes. But you know what?'

'What?'

'Change can be good too. You arriving here is a big change, and I'm sure glad you are here on our ship.'

I smiled so wide it made my cheeks hurt, and even then I kept smiling.

'Now I'm going to show you my favourite spot,' said Captain Jane. 'Follow me up here.' We wound up and up a metal staircase until we emerged in an all-glass room that sat on top of the ship like a hat.

'Whoa,' I said as I tried to look everywhere all at once. Outside, stars and planets whizzed by – or I suppose we whizzed by them. It was incredible.

'Welcome to the viewing platform,' said Captain Jane. 'If I'm not driving the ship, this is where you can usually find me. I do my best thinking up here, among the stars.'

We sat in friendly silence for a few moments, watching the stars and planets and meteors all around us. Something strange caught my eye, a kind of orange sparkling dust that was leaving a trail like a comet tail. But before I could ask Captain Jane about it, an alarm started blaring. I covered my ears.

'What is that?'

'I put in an alert for any planets that were out of orbit, and it looks like we are about

FUN FACT!

The largest meteor crater on Earth is the Vredefort crater in South Africa. It is 99 miles wide and was created around 2 billion years ago!

to hit another one!' said Captain Jane, racing back towards the command centre.

'Maybe we should land on this planet!' I said, dashing after her. 'It's strange that another planet is out of orbit, right?'

'It certainly is,' said Captain Jane. 'Quick, get into your space chair! You too, Spaceman Jack and Five-Eyed Frank!'

'You got it, Captain,' said Spaceman Jack.

'We aren't going to land just because she told us to, are we?' groaned Five-Eyed Frank, as he fastened his seat belt.

'Well, maybe on this planet there will be another clue for what happened to Planet Cheddar's moon!' I said. It was another opportunity to investigate, and as a scientist, I knew we needed more data.

And I'd get to explore another new planet!

'What planet is it anyway?' said Spaceman Jack, glancing out of the window. 'I wasn't paying attention to the flight plan.'

'Topsy-Turvy,' said Captain Jane.

'Oh no,' groaned Spaceman Jack. 'Not Topsy-Turvy! The last time we stopped there I was space sick for a whole week after!'

'As Suzie said, this is a great chance to get more information,' said Captain Jane. 'It can't be a coincidence that Topsy-Turvy is out of orbit too.'

She pulled on the controls and I felt TUBS begin to descend.

'And the good news is that Topsy-Turvy has similar oxygen levels to Earth and isn't a poisonous gas planet, so we don't need to wear our space helmets,' Captain Jane went on.

'The bad news is that the entire planet

is upside down, so be ready to feel very
dizzy,' said Spaceman Jack glumly.
'I can handle anything but
space sickness.'

'What do you mean upside
down?' I asked.

'Oh, you'll see.'

*

As we approached Topsy-Turvy, I frowned.
'Why are those clouds blue and green?'

'Those aren't clouds. Those are its
oceans. The water is in the sky. We'll have
to fly through it. Nothing TUBS can't handle.'

'The whole planet is bundled in a layer
of water like wrapping paper around a
present.' Spaceman Jack shook his head
and sighed deeply. 'And of course the
clouds are on the bottom. Oh, I hate this
planet.'

We blasted through the water and I pressed my nose to the window, trying to take it all in. We were going so fast I wasn't able to see much. It was like being on the fastest submarine ever!

Then we shot out of the water layer and Captain Jane expertly landed the ship. I peered out of the window. Spaceman Jack was right. There were clouds everywhere, forming up out of the ground.

I watched in awe as rain began to pour from one of the clouds and float up towards the water sky.

Then I saw a strange silvery creature floating through the mist, coming straight for the ship!

'What is *that*?'

The silvery creature had two huge heads on either side of its body, one on top and

one on bottom. And it had eight legs
wriggling in between. It looked like a two-
headed octopus! I watched as it scuttled
around, and then flipped over.

'They have a head on either end so
that way they are always right side up,'
explained Captain Jane.

'Or always upside down,' added
Spaceman Jack. 'Depends on how you look
at it.' Then he sighed. 'All right, let's go talk
to that floptopus and see what it knows.
But be careful, they have a tendency to be
a little unpredictable, depending
on which head you're talking to.

They aren't anywhere near as friendly as the babbits.'

'I'm going to stay in the spaceship,' announced Five-Eyed Frank. 'You know how I feel about floptopuses. They think they are sooooo special with their two heads. Well, I have five eyes. And Tommy has *three* heads!' He rolled all of his eyes.

'Floptopus?' I repeated, still trying to figure out the name.

'Yes, because look how they move.' Spaceman Jack pointed as the creature flip-flopped head over head on its way towards the ship.

'Ohhh! Floptopus. I get it,' I said. Then I grinned. I was about to meet my third alien of the day!

CHAPTER 10

TOPSY-TURVY

The ground on Topsy-Turvy was sturdier than the ground on Planet Cheddar, but that was the only thing stable about it.

Trees grew upside down, their roots reaching for the sky, and their branches and leaves burrowing down into the ground below.

Rain fell up, not down. And of course it started raining as soon as we exited the ship. The clouds gathered on the ground, and we had to wade through them, batting away raindrops. I wished I had worn my space helmet, just to keep the rain from going up my nose.

And I didn't like not being able to see my feet. It made me nervous, like I was going to step into a hole, or fall into a tunnel, like I had on Planet Cheddar.

The silver floptopus we'd spotted from TUBS glared at us with one head, and had a wide smile on the other. The glaring head was on top though, so I suspected that was how it was actually feeling.

'Halt!' cried the frowning head.

'Hello!' called the welcoming one.

I paused, staring at the strange creature. 'What are we supposed to do?' I whispered to Captain Jane. 'Which head do we listen to?'

'It will flip-flop in a moment,' she whispered back. 'They change their moods as quickly as the wind changes direction.'

'I don't like humans!' said the frowning head.

'But I do!' the welcoming head grinned at us.

'I'm on top right now,' the grumpy head snapped back.

'For now,' said the welcoming one.

'Oh, I feel so dizzy already,' moaned Spaceman Jack.

There was a squelching sound next to me and I nearly leaped out of my space boots as another floptopus landed right by my foot, one of its heads rising up out of the cloud. It was a dark purple, with glowing yellow veins.

'Hello, small human,' it said, eyeing me. I couldn't see its other head, but I knew it was near my feet. I hoped I wouldn't kick it accidentally. I had a feeling neither of its heads would like that.

'Hello,' I said.

Suddenly it upended itself and flopped over in front of me, the head that had just been on the ground now right side up, and the head I'd been talking to on the ground. The eight legs waved around, and one tapped me on the shoulder.

I could see why Five-Eyed Frank was not a fan of these aliens.

'Are you the one who put my planet to sleep?' it said suspiciously.

The silvery floptopus heard the question

and came flopping over. Luckily when it landed, the more friendly head was on top.

'What? No! I'm just a human girl. I don't have that kind of power!'

'Hmmm,' said both of the floptopuses in unison.

'So your entire planet is asleep except for you two?' I said. It was like the babbits on Planet Cheddar!

'Exactly,' said the purple one. 'Which is why we thought YOU were behind it.'

'Well, I'm not. I want to help you!' I insisted.

Spaceman Jack jogged over next to me and nodded at the two floptopuses. 'Hello, Pom and Mop,' he said to the purple one. I assumed he was addressing both of its heads. 'And hello Nip and Pin,' he said to the silver one. 'Nice to see all of you.

Listen, we were hoping you could help us out with something . . .'

The friendly silver floptopus, the one called Nip and Pin, flipped around. Its other head was now not just grumpy and suspicious, it was mad.

'Of course you are! You only ever come to our planet when you need something! Greedy human.'

'And the human girl was just claiming she was here to help *us*!' said the purple one, Pom and Mop.

Spaceman Jack held up his hands. 'Hey, hey, buddy. Calm down there. We *are* here to help. We noticed your planet is out of orbit.'

'Our planet is out of orbit?' said the purple floptopus. Without warning it flopped again. 'OUR PLANET IS OUT OF

ORBIT?' repeated the other head, much more panicked. I couldn't keep track which side was Pom and which was Mop.

'That's right – there is something strange going on. But we are going to figure out what it is! Did you see anything odd before the other floptopuses on your planet started falling asleep?'

The silver floptopus looked up at the sky. 'Well, the first thing I noticed was that something had stolen our moon.'

I gasped. Another missing moon!

But then when I looked up at the sky, I saw a moon. A big orange one.

'That isn't your moon?' I said, pointing at it.

The purple floptopus scoffed. 'That is clearly an inferior moon. Our moon is much nicer than that. Our moon has gone missing and has been replaced with that

131

thing. Barely even a moon! It is far too small!'

My thoughts began to go so fast I felt I could hardly keep up with them. I stared hard at the moon and realised it was rocking back and forth, like it was still settling into its new place in the sky. And drifting off it was that strange orange shimmery dust I'd seen from the viewing platform! It must have been moon dust!

'Wait!' I said. 'Is that the moon from Planet Cheddar?'

'Home of the babbits?' sneered the silver floptopus. 'We are far superior to those creatures.'

'Their moon went missing too,' I said. 'And I bet that moon is their moon!'

'But that doesn't make any sense,' said Spaceman Jack, frowning. 'Why would one moon replace another?'

'And why would moons disappearing put aliens to sleep?' said Captain Jane. 'How did you stay awake?'

The silver floptopus flipped again, and this time its head looked bashful. 'We were singing in the sound cave.'

'What's a sound cave?'

'THE BEST THING EVER,' squealed the purple floptopus. I wasn't sure which head I was talking to now, it had flopped so much I'd lost track. 'Your voice echoes back to you! It is the best way to practise singing.'

'We love singing.' And then the silver floptopus began to harmonise with itself. The purple one joined in and they sang the strangest song I'd ever heard. It sounded like how I imagine bubbles would sing, if bubbles had voices. It was airy and breathy and sort of tinkly too.

I clapped in appreciation.

'Very nice,' interrupted Captain Jane. 'But what does you being in the sound cave have to do with you staying awake?'

'It's a protected space,' explained the silver floptopus. 'When we are in there, we seal the cave shut for optimal acoustics.'

I frowned, trying to work out what he meant. And then it hit me. Acoustics had to do with sound. 'Oh!' I exclaimed. 'Like when my brother puts foam boards on the walls of the garage when he is recording a new song with his band.'

'I suppose so,' said the purple floptopus. 'But what is a garage?'

'Sort of like a cave,' I said with a smile. 'Like a cave where cars, erm, spaceships can park.'

'Intriguing,' said the silver one.

'So are you saying that the thing that put the planet to sleep did it using sound?' I said.

'Sound or light or even a poison gas. It is unclear what it was, but it did not reach us because we were in the sound cave,' said the purple one.

'Something strange is happening in our universe,' said Captain Jane. 'And we need to figure it out. One planet being put to sleep and going out of orbit is strange, two is a pattern.' She gazed up at the sky. 'And there could be more, for all we know.'

An idea suddenly hit me right on the head like a falling asteroid. 'We have to track down Topsy-Turvy's missing moon! It will lead us in the right direction,' I said. 'Think about it! We found Planet Cheddar's moon here. Doesn't it make sense that the

Topsy-Turvy moon will be at the next planet that is going to be put to sleep? And I bet that not only is the planet going to be put to sleep, but its moon is going to be stolen too!'

'Hmm,' said Captain Jane. 'You do have a point.'

'But don't we risk being put to sleep too?' said Spaceman Jack. 'I don't fancy falling asleep on a strange planet. I like to sleep in my sleep pod.'

'Well, there must be ways to protect ourselves from being put to sleep,' I said. 'Think about it. There were still four babbits awake on Planet Cheddar. And these two floptopuses stayed awake too. Whatever is putting everyone to sleep doesn't work perfectly. And if these two were protected by being in the sound cave, maybe we need to wear ear plugs on the next planet we go to.'

'The small human is talking sense,' said the purple floptopus. Then it flipped. 'I agree!' said its other head.

'I never knew it could be in agreement with itself,' whispered Spaceman Jack.

'Will you bring back our moon?' said the silver floptopus. 'This one smells of cheese.'

'Of course,' I said. 'We'll find your moon, bring it back, and return Planet Cheddar's moon to the babbits.'

'Really?' said the purple one, smiling with both heads.

'We'll do our best,' I said. I knew from my own experiments and inventions that results were never a sure thing, but I could at least guarantee we'd try as hard as we could. 'I promise.'

'Oh, there you go making promises again!' groaned Spaceman Jack.

'But we need one more thing from you,' I said, gazing up at the orange moon dust still slowly drifting off Planet Cheddar's moon. 'What colour is your moon?'

'Why purple and silver, of course,' said the purple floptopus.

'Why does the colour matter?' said Spaceman Jack.

I pointed up at a faint silver and purple swirl in the sky. 'Because we're going to follow that trail of moon dust.'

CHAPTER 11

CAKE, NAILS AND REHYDRATED CHICKEN

By the time we were back on TUBS, both the silver and purple floptopuses were smiley face up, and waving goodbye to us.

We blasted off, leaving the clouds on the ground with the upside-down trees, and went through the Topsy-Turvy sea-sky until we were back in space.

I was surprised how comfortable I already felt on the ship and with the crew (even Five-Eyed Frank). After all, it had only been one day. At least, I thought it had only been one day. It was hard to keep track of time while flying on a spaceship. On Earth, we track time by the Earth's rotation (24 hours) and how long it takes to go round the sun (365 days, or a year). In space, we didn't have anything like that. Time suddenly felt meaningless.

It made my head spin trying to think about it.

But I did know I was getting sleepy. And hungry.

'So . . . how do you keep track of time up here?' I asked, yawning. 'Time is different on different planets, right?'

'It is indeed,' said Captain Jane. She glanced at a blue clock on a wall next

FUN FACT!

The Earth's circumference is roughly 25 thousand miles and it rotates once every 24 hours. That means the Earth's surface at the equator is rotating at over a thousand miles per hour!

to a calendar. 'Barely any time at all has passed on Earth since you arrived.'

That was reassuring. At least my family wouldn't be too worried.

'TUBS is on its own time,' Captain Jane went on. 'And we've set it so that it alerts us when it is time to eat and sleep.'

'I never need reminding about when to eat,' said Spaceman Jack.

As if on cue a bell began ringing, and my stomach growled loudly.

'It is time for our feast,' said Captain Jane with a laugh. 'Come on!'

*

We all followed Captain Jane to the canteen. I pushed open the door and then gasped in delight.

There was a huge pink cake on the table!

'A CAKE!' yelled Five-Eyed Frank. 'And it

is pink! My favourite colour!'

'I thought you'd like that,' said Captain Jane with a smile. 'I made the icing using the strawberries.'

'IT LOOKS BEAUTIFUL!' cried Five-Eyed Frank as he bounced up and down in excitement, nearly hitting his head on the ceiling.

'I hope you like strawberry space cake, Suzie,' Captain Jane said to me.

'Who cares if *she* likes it?' said Five-Eyed Frank, all of his eyes looking at the cake. 'I LOVE IT!'

'I care if she likes it,' said Captain Jane, with a laugh. 'You can't even eat it!'

'But I can look at it! And it looks delicious!' said Five-Eyed Frank.

'I agree!' I said. 'I'm sure I'll love it.' I couldn't believe that Captain Jane had made a cake for me. Well, and for Five-Eyed Frank, even if he couldn't eat it.

'And this is also for you, Frank,' Captain Jane went on, and passed him a metal cup full of what looked like nails and screws. 'So you have something to actually eat.'

Wait. It *was* full of nails and screws.

And they were rusty.

'RUSTY NAILS!' Five-Eyed Frank opened his mouth and poured the whole thing in, chomping with joy. 'And worms!' He slurped up a still-wriggling worm. 'What a treat!'

'I've been soaking those nails in a bucket of saltwater for weeks,' said Captain Jane with a wide smile. 'This seemed like the perfect occasion.'

'Why saltwater?' I asked. 'And where did you even get salt water in space?' I knew that water and oxygen could make things rust (after all, I'd seen what had happened to Flipper the car) but I didn't know why Captain Jane had used saltwater.

'Well,' said Captain Jane. 'Saltwater speeds up the rust process because salt works as an electrolyte, which means the electrons can move more easily. And rusting is all about the movement of electrons, so iron rusts more quickly in saltwater.'

'What is an electron?'

'You don't know what an electron is?' said Five-Eyed Frank between slurps of nails.

'No,' I said. 'That's why I'm asking.'

Some people don't like not knowing things, but any time I don't know something, I see it as an opportunity. The more questions I ask, the more I know.

'Everything is made of atoms,' explained Spaceman Jack. 'They are really tiny particles you can't see without special equipment. And atoms are made of electrons, neutrons and protons. And when electrons jump from atom to atom, it creates electricity!'

'And what does that have to do with rusty nails?'

Nails are made out of iron, and when iron comes into contact with water and oxygen over a period of time, it leads to rust. The addition of salt, which is an electrolyte, increases the rate that the electrons can be transferred. The iron is losing electrons, and oxygen is gaining them.

'Whoa,' I said, my eyes wide. I'd never look at saltwater, or nails, or rust, the same again. Who knew so many things had to happen for something to rust? Captain Jane still hadn't answered all of my questions though. 'But where did you get the saltwater?'

'Oh, there's a water planet in the next solar system,' said Captain Jane. 'Last time we were there I filled up a bottle.'

'Is that the planet with the evil shark

lord?' I remembered seeing that episode of
Space Blasters!

'It *was* the planet with the evil shark
lord,' corrected Spaceman Jack. 'Happy
to say I defeated him and that planet is
peaceful once more.' He puffed out his
chest with pride, and beamed.

'Ahem. *We* defeated him,' said Captain
Jane.

'Yes, yes, that's what I meant,' said
Spaceman Jack quickly. He cleared his
throat. 'What else is on the menu for this
feast?'

'It's a space buffet!' Captain Jane held
up a selection of tinfoil bags. 'We've got
rehydrated chicken. Mashed potato! And
of course a few fresh veggies from the
greenhouse.'

'What is rehydrated chicken?' I asked.

'When we bring food on the ship, we have to dehydrate it – take out all the liquid – so it takes up less space and lasts longer. Then when we are ready to eat it, we add water to rehydrate it,' said Captain Jane.

'And if we are visiting a friendly planet, we always ask if we can stay for dinner,' said Spaceman Jack. 'Just to make our own supplies last longer.'

'What kind of food do you like to eat back at home, Suzie?' said Captain Jane as she put a piece of chicken and some mashed potatoes on my plate. I took a bite and was pleasantly surprised. It was chewy, and didn't taste like the chicken I had at home, but it was still pretty good.

'My favourite food is dumplings,' I said, and then I went on to explain about Po-Po's dumplings and what had happened with the ADM.

'I'd sure love to try one of your grandma's dumplings one day,' said Spaceman Jack. 'They sound great!'

'Maybe I can try and make them here,' I said, looking around the canteen for anything that might work for dumpling ingredients. Then I glanced at Five-Eyed Frank. 'I bet I could even make you a rusty-nail dumpling! The great thing about dumplings is you can put pretty much anything in them!'

I had no idea how I was going to make a rusty-nail dumpling, but I was determined to try.

'That . . . would be

nice,' said Five-Eyed Frank hesitantly. He gave me a puzzled look. 'Why would you do that?'

'Because if we are all having dumplings, I'd want you to have one too,' I said.

I thought this would make him happy, but he glowered at me. 'Don't pity me!'

'I'm not! I'm trying to be nice.'

'Well, don't! Just because I can't eat human food doesn't mean I need special treatment. I was here before you! And I'll be here after you too!'

'I'm not trying to take your place,' I said quietly. 'I just want to be your friend.'

'NOBODY CAN TAKE MY PLACE!' Five-Eyed Frank shrieked.

'That isn't what I meant,' I said, feeling tears of frustration prickle behind my eyes.

'Now why don't we cut that cake?' said
Spaceman Jack quickly. 'Frank, we'll even
save you a piece to look at.'

'Don't bother,' said Five-Eyed Frank and
then he stormed out of the canteen.

'Well,' said Spaceman Jack after a
moment. 'More cake for us.'

'Don't worry, Suzie,' said Captain Jane.
'Frank can be a little sensitive sometimes.
It isn't anything personal.'

'It sure feels personal,' I said as I stared
down at my piece of cake.

'Have some cake,' said Spaceman Jack.
'It'll make everything a little bit better.'

I took a bite and to my surprise, he was
right.

'We're really glad you're here,' said
Captain Jane. 'And Frank will come around.'

I nodded and took another bite of cake.

*

After dinner, I climbed into my sleep pod. It had its own little window looking out into the galaxy, and it was *incredible*. Stars swirled and danced as we zoomed past planets of all sizes and colours. We were still trying to track down the Topsy-Turvy moon by following the silver-purple moon dust. And Captain Jane thought that the tracker on TUBS had got a read on something strange, something that might have been the Topsy-Turvy moon, so we'd set a course to follow it for as long as it aligned with the silver-purple moon dust trail.

As I settled in my sleep pod, I realised how different it was from my bed at home. I hoped my parents weren't too worried about me. I wondered if my brother and

sister would even care that
I was gone. But I knew my gung-gung
and po-po would care. I was supposed to
be seeing them next weekend! Hopefully
I'd be home by then, and me and the
Space Blasters crew would have solved the
mystery of the missing moons and figured
out why entire planets were falling asleep.

'I'm sure I'll be back home soon,'
I whispered, my fingers on the window, as
if my words could travel through space all
the way down to my family.

Then I closed my eyes, and let the
rumbling of the spaceship lull me to sleep.

*Sleep, small human. Sleep. Sleep and
dream. What do you dream of? Dumplings?
Mmm, delicious. Yes, your dreams are
delicious. Stay asleep. Stay dreaming.
Argh – this spaceship is too fast! Wait!
Slow down! No, don't wake up . . . keep
dreaming of dumplings. Oh, and of cake
too! Oh no, you are waking up . . .*

I sat bolt upright and bonked my head
on the roof of my sleep pod. 'Ow!' I said,
rubbing it.

I'd been having the strangest dream.
I couldn't remember it all, but there was a
voice, and it was talking about dumplings.
That was it! I was dreaming about
dumplings. But the details weren't clear.
My brain felt fuzzy, like someone had been
rummaging around in it.

And something had woken me up.
I glanced out of the window and gasped.
We were going so fast the stars had turned
into blurs!

What was *that*? It looked like lavender
clouds were trailing TUBS, even hanging on
to the side, almost like giant fingers. And
were those . . . eyes? Or burning stars?

I squinted, trying to make sense of what
I was seeing, and then suddenly there
was a roaring in my ears, like someone
shouting, but before I could make out what

they were saying, TUBS picked up even more speed, and the lavender cloud blew off into space.

'*I have to tell Captain Jane about that,*' I thought, and tried to sit up, but I was so tired. So, *so* sleepy. '*I'll tell her in the morning,*' I thought. '*Must remember.*' And then, before my head even hit my pillow, I was asleep again.

CHAPTER 12

KNOTS

I woke up the next morning with a terrible headache. My brain felt fuzzy and I had a bump on my head.

'Weird,' I said, rubbing my head. I couldn't remember hitting it, but I must have in my sleep.

'It might be a bit of space lag,' said Captain Jane at breakfast when I told her about it. 'Kind of like jet lag but way worse.'

'Here, have some super smoothie,' said

Spaceman Jack, pushing a very green drink towards me.

I wrinkled my nose. 'What is in it?'

'A bunch of vegetables from the greenhouse, vitamins, all good stuff. I drink a glass every day and it keeps me fit as a fiddle!'

'Spaceman Jack is right, you should stay hydrated. It will help with your headache.'

'OK,' I said, taking a tentative sip of the mystery green drink. Yuck. It tasted like hay mixed with broccoli.

'You know,' said Captain Jane, sipping her own green smoothie. 'I didn't sleep very well last night either. I kept tossing and turning. And TUBS unexpectedly went into hyperspeed.' She knocked on the side of the ship. 'Hey, TUBS, why did you go into hyperspeed?'

'**There was an interference with the ship,**' said TUBS in its robotic voice. '**Something was trying to catch us.**'

My eyes widened. 'That sounds . . . alarming.'

'Oh, nothing to worry about,' said Spaceman Jack cheerfully. 'Probably some space debris. Or might have been a floating alien trying to hitch-hike a ride on the side of the spaceship. That happens sometimes. But TUBS is too smart and too fast.'

'**It was an unknown entity,**' said TUBS. '**There will be photos on my main drive.**'

'Perfect,' said Captain Jane. 'That will at least solve one mystery.'

*

But it didn't. The photos just showed what looked like a big, fluffy cloud, too blurry to see anything else clearly.

'Look, Suzie,' said Captain Jane.
'Whatever it was, it was closest to your
sleep-pod window. Did you see anything?'

I scrunched my eyes shut and tried to
remember.

'I can't even remember my dreams from
last night,' I said. 'I must have been fast
asleep.'

'Hmm,' said Captain Jane. 'Now that you
mention it, I can't remember my dreams
either. And I usually do.'

Before she could say more, an alarm
went off overhead, flashing red and white
lights.

**'TOPSY-TURVY MOON IS IN RANGE.
MOON AHEAD AND HEADING FOR
NEAREST PLANET.'**

'Jumpin' Jupiter, we've found it!' said

Spaceman Jack.

'Everyone in your chairs!' said Captain Jane. 'We're making an unexpected landing!'

'Where to?' I asked in excitement as I ran to my space chair.

'A new planet for us,' said Captain Jane, pressing buttons on the control panel.

'Knot,' said Five-Eyed Frank who was next to me. It was the first thing he'd said to me since he'd stormed out of the canteen.

'Not what?'

'No, Knot.'

I sighed. I knew Five-Eyed Frank wasn't my biggest fan but he didn't need to make things more difficult on purpose.

'The planet is called Knot.'

That still wasn't very helpful. 'Like not

there, but here? Or not this, but that?'

'No. Like a knot in a rope.'

'Ohhh! Why is it called that?'

Five-Eyed Frank glanced out of the
window. 'From the looks of it, because it is
a very knotty planet.'

I looked out too and gasped. The whole
planet looked like a giant ball of red wool, all
tangled up. No wonder it was called Knot!

'What do we know
about the life
forms there?'
called
Spaceman
Jack. 'Come
on, Frankie,
you are our
resident alien
expert.'

'I am an alien. Not an alien expert,' said Five-Eyed Frank tersely. 'And you know I do not care for that nickname.'

'Aha! So we've found an alien you don't know anything about,' said Spaceman Jack. 'Bound to happen eventually. Don't feel bad.'

'Of course I know about the tangles of Knot!' Five-Eyed Frank burst out.

'Knew it!' crowed Spaceman Jack. 'Give us the intel.'

Five-Eyed Frank sighed deeply. 'They are elusive and extremely hard to find. And they apparently blend in very well with their natural surroundings.'

'I can always track down an alien,' said Spaceman Jack. 'One of my special skills.'

'And the Topsy-Turvy moon is headed towards this planet?' I said, eager to be part of the conversation.

'It's already arrived,' said Five-Eyed Frank. 'Look.'

'That's the moon?' It looked like a spinning top over Planet Knot. 'I didn't know moons spun like that. It's making me dizzy.'

'What else would you expect from Topsy-Turvy?' grumbled Spaceman Jack.

'And the addition of a new moon is already knocking Knot out of orbit. But it looks like the planet's other moon is still there,' said Captain Jane, pointing at a huge blue moon. 'Which means we can witness if it disappears! Get ready for landing, everyone. And remember – our goal is to figure out why the Topsy-Turvy moon is here, and make sure the Knot moon doesn't disappear!'

'Captain,' said Five-Eyed Frank, sounding

more anxious than I'd ever heard him, which was saying something because he always sounded anxious.

'You have to watch out for the tangles! The more worried they get, the more their hair tangles in their surroundings, and anything caught in their way will get tangled up with them, so before you know it, you'll be stuck on Knot forever!'

'Not going to happen,' said Spaceman Jack, brandishing a pair of scissors.

'Don't say I didn't warn you . . .' said Five-Eyed Frank. 'But I'm staying on the ship!'

'Frankie, my friend, you always stay on the ship,' said Spaceman Jack.

'And it's a good thing he does,' said Captain Jane. 'We need someone to look after TUBS.'

Five-Eyed Frank beamed with pride. 'Exactly! It is the MOST important job.'

'Well, I wouldn't say most important,' said Spaceman Jack. 'Doing the exploring and meeting the aliens is also pretty important, you know.'

'You're both extremely important,' said Captain Jane in a voice that sounded like she'd said this a million times before. 'Now let's go find out what is happening on Knot.'

*

When I flew down the space chute, this time I was prepared. As soon as my feet hit the ground, I leaped up.

But I wasn't fast enough. Two long ropes of hair grabbed me by the ankles.

'Argh!' I cried.

Spaceman Jack was next down the chute, and he quickly hacked away at the hair. It slithered off like a moving thing, and I shuddered.

Then a mound of bright yellow hair rolled right towards us. It looked like tumbleweed made of hair. As it came closer I saw it had huge eyes peering out from underneath all the hair.

'Not from Knot!' it declared.

The ground began to rumble and more and more of the yellow hairballs (because that is the best way to explain what they looked like) rolled towards us, until we were surrounded.

'Erm, I thought Five-Eyed Frank said these guys were hard to find,' said Spaceman Jack.

'Hello, tangles,' said Captain Jane. 'We're sorry we have arrived without warning. But we are trying to figure out why you have a

new moon.' She pointed up at the Topsy-Turvy moon in the sky, which was still spinning rapidly.

The tangles all moved as one, staring up at the sky.

'And have any of you fallen asleep recently?' I added, eager to help. 'I mean, unexpectedly.'

The tangles shook back and forth in what I interpreted as a no.

'But where has our moon gone?' said one. The others began to repeat after it. 'Our moon is gone! Where is our moon? Not our moon! Not the Knot moon! Knot moon is much bigger!' The tangles began to bounce anxiously, and as they did, their hair grew longer and longer, and began to tie itself to the hair covering Knot.

'Thunderin' asteroids, we missed another

moon snatch!' cried Spaceman Jack. 'How did that happen?'

It was true! The Knot blue moon that had just been next to the Topsy-Turvy moon was gone!

One of the tangles began to yawn, and it made me yawn too. I suddenly felt so sleepy I had to sit down. Luckily the floor of Knot was so soft. It was like the comfiest bed ever. I felt a gentle tug on my own hair, like someone was braiding it.

'Suzie! Get up!' cried a voice, but it was from so far away.

'Just going to close my eyes for a second,' I said. One of the tangles rolled towards me and I realised its hair was wrapping up in mine.

Oh no! We'd been so distracted by seeing the moon on Planet Knot that we had forgotten our plan to protect ourselves from falling asleep!

I began to pull against the hair ropes, but the harder I pulled the more tangled they became.

And with every moment that passed, I felt sleepier, and sleepier. I had to wake up. Otherwise I'd be stuck on Knot forever and I'd never get home!

Were the tangles somehow responsible for putting all the planets to sleep?

But that was impossible, because as I forced my eyes open, I saw that they were falling asleep too, and rolling away or getting caught in the hair of Knot.

'WAKE UP, SUZIE!' yelled a voice right in my ear and as I sat straight up I yowled in pain because my hair was even more tangled with Knot.

And to my surprise, I found myself staring right into two of Five-Eyed Frank's eyes.

'YOU HAVE TO RELAX!' he said, in the least relaxed voice I'd ever heard. All of his eyes were wide and panicked. 'That is the only way the hair grips will loosen.'

I took a few deep, calming breaths and tried to think happy thoughts. Slowly, I felt

Knot release its hold on me, and as soon as it was loose enough, Five-Eyed Frank pulled me up.

Most of the tangles had fallen asleep, and only a few were still awake, bouncing in panic and getting more and more tangled.

'Where's Captain Jane?' I cried. 'And Spaceman Jack?'

Five-Eyed Frank shook his head and pointed at his ears. I realised he was wearing giant earmuffs that I hadn't noticed in my panic.

But he must have understood what I said because he pointed at the ground and I saw Spaceman Jack and Captain Jane both sound asleep, and completely tied up in Knot hair!

I gasped and moved towards them, but

it felt like I was moving through syrup. I was suddenly so sleepy again. There was a strange music in the air, almost like a song, and it was so soothing, so, so soothing. I just needed to sit down again, and maybe close my eyes.

Then Five-Eyed Frank thrust a pair of headphones on me, and his voice rang out in my ears, even louder than the song, snapping me awake.

'Don't you dare go to sleep, human! I need your help! The whole universe does!' As he spoke he shook me by the shoulders. 'Stay awake, I say!'

I nodded. 'I will! But we have to wake up Spaceman Jack and Captain Jane too!'

'I know that,' he snapped.

Something overhead caught my eye. 'Wait! What is THAT?'

It was a huge lavender cloud, with big orange eyes and long, reaching fingers. It looked like an ancient tree crossed with a fluffy cloud. And it was racing around on a huge blue moon! The Knot moon!

Wait . . . I'd seen that lavender thing before. Outside my window! It had tried to put me to sleep! Just like it was trying to put everyone to sleep now.

'We have to catch that moon-snatcher!' I cried to Five-Eyed Frank. Together we untangled Captain Jane and Spaceman Jack, but we couldn't wake them up.

'What are we going to do?' Five-Eyed Frank cried. 'The moon-snatcher is getting away!'

CHAPTER 13

THE CHASE

'We have to get back to the ship!' I cried.

'We can't leave Spaceman Jack and Captain Jane!' said Five-Eyed Frank.

'I know that,' I said. 'But I don't know how to get them back! They're too heavy for us to carry!'

Then I realised something. They might have been too heavy for us to carry if we were on Earth, but maybe the gravity was different on Planet Knot? I tentatively crouched down and tried to pick up Captain

Jane. My arms trembled with effort but I was able to do it!

'Wow!' said Five-Eyed Frank. 'You are stronger than you look.'

'The gravity is working in our favour,' I said. 'I bet you can carry Spaceman Jack!'

'He's five times my size!' squealed Five-Eyed Frank.

'I have an idea!' I quickly yanked several long, thick hairs up from Knot, and used them to tie Spaceman Jack and Captain Jane to each other back to back. 'Now we can carry them together!'

'If you say so,' said Five-Eyed Frank doubtfully.

'Do you have any better ideas?' I demanded. I knew Five-Eyed Frank didn't like me very much, but we didn't have time for this.

'No,' sniffed Five-Eyed Frank. 'I just don't know if it will work.'

'We have to try! Here, you take their feet and I'll pick up their heads.'

'Hey! It's working!'

'Hurry!'

Working together, we carried Spaceman Jack and Captain Jane back to the ship, and we only dropped them once.

When we were back on the ship, we untied them and lay them down in the middle of the command centre. Tommy flew over and chirped anxiously. He landed next to Spaceman Jack and nudged his face with one of his heads.

Spaceman Jack kept sleeping.

Tommy chirped louder, using all three of his mouths, and still Spaceman Jack kept sleeping. So did Captain Jane.

'Now what?' I said.

Five-Eyed Frank ran to the canteen and came back with a cup of water. He threw it on them, and they still kept sleeping.

I swallowed. What were we going to do? I wracked my brain, and then remembered the strange song, and the lavender cloud

with fingers. 'That thing, that thing we saw.
It must be what put them to sleep! I bet
if we catch it, we can convince it to wake
them up too.'

'But how will we catch it if we're stuck
here on Planet Knot? We need Captain Jane
to fly the ship!'

I looked at Five-Eyed Frank. 'I bet you
could fly the ship.'

He was so shocked he nearly fell over.

'Me?'

'Yes, you! You've seen Captain Jane do it
hundreds of times, right?'

He nodded, all his eyes wide.

'And you said before that TUBS can
practically fly itself.'

He nodded again.

'You'd just be steering, really. And I bet
you'd be good at that, since you can see in

so many different directions.'

'Do you really think I can do it?' Five-Eyed Frank said in a quiet voice.

'No,' I said, and his face fell. 'I don't *think* you can – I know you can!'

He beamed at me. 'OK. I'll do it!'

The mechanical voice of TUBS whirred to life. '**Do not worry, Five-Eyed Frank. You know me as well as Captain Jane does. You can fly me.**'

'Well, that settles it then!' I said. 'Time to fly!'

*

Moments later, we were ready for take-off. In the distance we could just barely see the giant blue Knot moon with the strange lavender creature on it.

'All right, Frank, are you ready?'

Five-Eyed Frank nodded from Captain

Jane's seat. '**FOR THE UNIVERSE!**' he said.

'**FOR THE UNIVERSE!**' And then we
took off and were zooming through the sky
after the cloud creature.

'What do you think it is?' I said as I tried
to get a better look at it. 'And what was
it doing outside our ship the other night?'
Because now I was certain it was what I'd
seen, and what I'd heard in my sleep too!
The strange dream had come back to me
after I saw it and heard its song.

'I've never seen anything like it,' said
Five-Eyed Frank. 'Here, pull up the alien
database on that screen in front of you,
and type in what we know.'

I followed Five-Eyed Frank's instructions,
and then the database projected an image
that looked just like the thing we were
chasing.

'**Dream-eater alien,**' said a robotic voice.

Five-Eyed Frank gasped. 'I didn't think those were real!'

'An alien that eats dreams?' I said. 'But why would it do that?'

'The same reason anyone eats anything,' said Five-Eyed Frank. 'It's what they need to stay alive. It would be like if you were called a food-eater human.' Then he frowned. 'But they are meant to be non-threatening. It says here that they usually only eat excess dreams, from sleepers who have so many dreams they don't miss a few. And they are supposed to be much, much smaller too.'

'Well, that one is *huge*. It's even bigger than it was the other night!' I said, craning my neck to get a better view of it. 'And how is it riding that moon like a racehorse?'

'It must have figured out how to power moons like some sort of personal spaceship,' said Five-Eyed Frank. 'I'd be impressed if I wasn't so irritated that it's causing such havoc in the universe!'

Something occurred to me. 'Wait! Have all the missing moons been bigger than the last?'

Five-Eyed Frank nodded.

'I THINK I HAVE A HYPOTHESIS ABOUT THE MOONS!' I was so excited I was shouting, but I couldn't stop – I had to get my idea out before it floated away.

The dream-eater alien is somehow putting entire planets to sleep so it can gorge on their dreams! And then it gets too big for the moon it is flying on, so it needs to steal a bigger one to ride around on!

'Thundering asteroids, I think you might be right!' said Five-Eyed Frank.

I laughed. 'You sound like Spaceman Jack!'

'Some of his sayings are pretty catchy,' said Five-Eyed Frank. 'And speaking of catchy, we've got to catch that thing! It keeps outpacing us.' Then he gave me an anxious look. 'If your theory is correct, what is going to stop it from putting the whole universe to sleep forever so it can always eat dreams?'

I gulped. 'Nothing at all. We've got to stop it!'

*

We raced through space, but the dream-eater alien was always just ahead of us.

'It will have to stop to feed on more dreams eventually,' said Five-Eyed Frank, his mouth set in a determined line.

'That's it!' I cried. 'I know how to catch it!'

I told Five-Eyed Frank my plan.

'Do you really think that will work?' he said. 'And can you actually build something to amplify Jane and Jack's dreams enough to tempt the dream-eater alien to our ship?'

'Of course I can!' I said confidently. I had to believe in myself, otherwise nobody else would, clearly. Then I frowned. 'Why don't you trust me?'

Five-Eyed Frank sighed. 'It isn't personal. I'm naturally anxious. All the aliens from my planet are. But if you say you can do that, I believe you.' He gave me a wide grin. 'After all, you're an inventor, aren't you?'

I beamed. 'You bet I am!' I was sure I could do this. I had to. My crew *and* the universe was depending on me.

Luckily the Gadget Room had an excellent supply closet. There was everything I needed to make the Dream Amplifier. I used tinfoil, some wires, a light bulb, a fan, two metal buckets and a high-powered radio for my invention. I hooked it up to Captain Jane and Spaceman Jack.

'This should work,' I said. 'They should hopefully already be dreaming.'

'Sounds good, Suzie the Inventor,' said Five-Eyed Frank.

'That sounds way better than Suzie the Spy,' I said with a grin.

'What are you going to do when it comes?' said Five-Eyed Frank. 'Have you thought about that?'

'Don't worry,' I said. 'I've got a plan for what to do when the dream-eater alien comes. And it will come. It won't be able to resist their delicious dreams.'

'Hey, Suzie?'

I looked over at Five-Eyed Frank. 'Yeah?'

'This was a good idea.'

I felt a warm glow go through me at Five-Eyed Frank's words. It felt like we were finally starting to become friends.

CHAPTER 14

EVEN ALIENS GET LONELY

'INCOMING!' Five-Eyed Frank yelled from the front of the ship. 'WE'VE GOT A VISITOR! A BIG, FLUFFY DREAM-EATING VISITOR!'

'I'm ready!' I still had my headphones on, so it wouldn't be able to put me to sleep.

I watched out of the window as the dream-eater alien approached on its flying moon. It was even bigger than the last time. It reached out for TUBS, and the whole spaceship shuddered as its long, gnarled fingers gripped on.

The dream-eater alien put a giant eye up to the spaceship window and stared at me.

'Hello,' I said. It blinked back at me.

'Would you like to try some cake?' I said. 'You have to promise you won't put me to sleep.'

The dream-eater alien blinked again. And then it nodded.

'I think you are too big to fit in here,' I said. 'But I can come out to you.'

*

Five minutes later, I was in my spacesuit and had the space rope secured around my waist to keep me from floating off. Five-Eyed Frank double-checked my helmet was secured and my air supply was working.

I was going on my first spacewalk. I very

carefully opened the hatch in the exit room, and suddenly there was no gravity. I flew up into the air, and out into outer space.

The dream-eater alien was waiting for me. It poked its giant head up over the spaceship. It was so big now, it could have played with TUBS like a toy. I gulped, but was determined to stick to my plan.

I held out what was left of the strawberry cake. As I let go, it began to float too. The dream-eater alien reached out and grabbed it, inspecting it curiously.

'I don't know if you can actually eat it,' I admitted. 'Five-Eyed Frank can't. But you can look at it. And you can try to eat it.'

'I have had cake in dreams,' it said, its

voice low and rumbly. 'But never cake I can put in my mouth. I will try.'

It popped the piece of pink cake in its mouth and chewed. 'It is delicious! Even better than dream cake!'

'I'm glad.' Then I put on my most serious face. 'Dream-eater alien, you have to stop putting planets to sleep. I know you eat dreams, but that doesn't excuse what you are doing. You are putting the whole universe into chaos! Especially because you keep stealing moons and sending planets out of orbit.'

The dream-eater alien's mouth wobbled like it was going to cry.

'What is it?' I said gently.

'I'm so lonely!' wailed the dream-eater alien. 'I had a friend once, an alien just like me, but they moved to another galaxy.

And when I eat dreams, I can meet other creatures! And explore new worlds! And try new foods! Otherwise I'm stuck on my own moon all alone. I'm the only dream-eater alien in the whole galaxy. I don't have any friends.'

'Ohhhh!' I said. 'I understand. My best friend Bonnie moved away, and so did my grandparents, and my brother and sister are always too busy to hang out with me. It's hard being lonely. But you can always make new friends.'

A fat lavender tear rolled down the dream-eater's cloud face. 'I didn't mean to hurt anyone. Taking the dreams doesn't hurt them.'

'No, but putting them to sleep forever does,' I said. 'Here, have some more cake, it will cheer you up.'

The dream-eater alien accepted the cake.

'You have to stop putting planets to sleep just so you can gorge on dreams,' I said. 'You can still eat dreams when the creatures are asleep, like you are meant to, but only when they go to sleep naturally. Oh, and you have to stop stealing moons.'

The dream-eater alien chewed on some cake in silence.

'And guess what?' I said. 'If you aren't always putting people to sleep, you can meet them in real life! And then you won't be so lonely either. It will be even better than eating dreams.'

'Will you be my friend, small human with the cake?' said the dream-eater alien.

I nodded. 'I'd love to be your friend. You can visit me in my dreams whenever you want, and I can tell you about my new inventions. And I can try to help you send a message to your friend who moved! I bet Captain Jane and Spaceman Jack will want to be your friend too. And the babbits! And the floptopuses! There are so many friends to be found in the universe.'

'Do you think everyone will forgive me for stealing their moons and putting them to sleep?'

'They will if you return the moons and say you're sorry,' I said. 'I know it will be hard. But it will be worth it.'

The dream-eater alien let out a huge breath.

'Do you know, small human, that this is the nicest anyone has ever been to me? Other than my best friend, of course. But other than them nobody has ever given me a present or even wanted to talk to me. And you brought me cake. I don't feel so lonely any more.'

'Dream-eater alien, you are going to have so many friends. When you return the moons and wake everyone up, you'll be a hero! And everyone always wants to be friends with a hero.'

SUZIE SAVES THE UNIVERSE

'We couldn't have done it without you,'
said Captain Jane. 'You saved the universe,
Suzie.'

The dream-eater alien had stayed true
to its word and had woken up Captain Jane
and Spaceman Jack. Five-Eyed Frank and
I had quickly told them what happened,
and they'd been shocked, and impressed.
Now we were up on the viewing platform,
waving goodbye to the dream-eater alien
as it prepared to go wake up everyone else

it had put to sleep, and return the moons. It was already shrinking back to its normal size, so it would be able to fit on its original moon.

'Come back soon and I'll make you dumplings!' I cried out to it before it flew off into space in the direction of Planet Knot.

'How did you know it was lonely?' asked Five-Eyed Frank.

I shrugged. 'I just had a feeling.'

'That doesn't sound very scientific,' said Five-Eyed Frank.

'No, but sometimes we have to trust our feelings too,' I said.

'And I'm glad you did,' said Spaceman Jack. 'Usually I'm the one who saves the day, but you know what? It was nice being saved too.'

'All I did was talk to the alien,' I said, blushing. 'I wouldn't say I saved the day.'

'But you did! You used your kindness and your creativity, and now the entire universe is saved, Suzie.' Captain Jane saluted me. 'We could use someone like you all the time on the ship, you know.'

I felt my heart leap. Part of me wanted to stay on TUBS forever, but the other part of me knew I had to get back home.

'But as much as I wish you would stay,' Captain Jane went on, 'you kept your promise to help the aliens we met, and now it's time for me to keep my promise to you. Time to figure out how to get you home.'

Just then TUBS began blaring an alarm. **'SUSPICIOUS ACTIVITY AHEAD!'** it said. **'SUSPICIOUS ACTIVITY DETECTED!'**

We looked out into space to see what TUBS had detected. We were heading right towards a new planet, one I hadn't seen before.

'Do you really have to go home right now?' said Five-Eyed Frank, hopping around.

'You can't help with our next mission?'

'Well,' I said. 'Maybe I could stay on a little bit longer . . .'

'That's the spirit!' cried Spaceman Jack.

'After all,' said Captain Jane, 'the universe still needs you.'

'I'd like you to stay,' said Five-Eyed Frank. 'We make a pretty good team.'

'We'll take you right home after this next mission,' said Spaceman Jack. 'And with your help, we'll be done faster than the speed of light!'

'But it's your choice, Suzie,' said Captain Jane.

I looked out of the window and thought about it. My family would understand if I stayed in space just a little bit longer . . .

I grinned. '**FOR THE UNIVERSE!**' I declared. 'I'll stay for one more mission.'

The Space Blasters crew cheered and we shot off into the stars. It was time to save the universe, again!

POSTCARD

Hi Bonnie!
Guess what? I've been sucked
into the show SPACE BLASTERS,
and now they need my help to
save the universe! I've been to
three new planets, and met lots
of aliens! I'm having a great
time, but I wish you were with
me. Hope you are having fun in
New York. I miss you!
Suzie

Bonnie

New York

Earth

COMING SOON . . .

SPACE BLASTERS

SUZIE AND THE MOON BUGS

Acknowledgements

We are over the moon to have the best team in the entire universe working on SPACE BLASTERS! There is a whole awesome crew of people to thank.

First, we'd like to thank Claire Wilson, our agent, for being the captain of our publishing career and never steering us wrong. We'd also like to thank Safae El-Ouahabi at RCW for her assistance and support.

We love working with everyone at Farshore! We would especially like to thank our superstar editors Liz Bankes and Lindsey Heaven, and welcome Asmaa Isse to the Space Blasters crew! We would also like to thank Aleena Hasan for her work on the book, and on the marketing and PR side, we are so appreciative to Pippa Poole, Hannah Penny, Jas Bansal and Ellie Bavester. Total dream team!

We'll be honest, our favourite part of SPACE BLASTERS are the incredible

illustrations and amazing cover art! And for that we have to thank Ryan Hammond, the best designer in the universe, and the phenomenally talented illustrator Amy Nguyen. Thank you for bringing Suzie and the crew to life so perfectly.

And a huge thank you to the booksellers, librarians and teachers who have introduced our books to young readers around the world! Speaking of young readers, a special hello to Diego and Leonel Garcia, and Will Scott, for being fans of our books.

Of course, we have to thank our wonderful families for their ongoing support and love. Thank you to our Tsang, Webber, Hopper and Liu relatives all over Planet Earth. Special thanks to Katie's siblings Jack and Jane for letting us steal their names. We also want to give a shout-out to Kevin's sister Stephanie (who inspired a certain space turtle) and our nephew Cooper.

This book is dedicated to our daughters, Evie and Mira, who light up our lives and inspire us every day.